MW01443779

The Beauty Within This Beast- Book Five: Caparina

By Lisa Craddock

This book is lovingly dedicated to all the Capricorns who have graced my life. I have been blessed with so many of you that choosing just one to honor here felt almost impossible. In the end, I decided to dedicate this to the very first Capricorn I ever met—Ardell Times-Simmons, my first cousin.

Ardell, you are the only person I have ever known who is genuinely happy every time she sees me, no matter the circumstance. Your unwavering warmth and joy have left an indelible mark on my heart. I regret the years we've spent apart, but I hold onto the hope of the many more years we have yet to share. Thank you for being the beautiful, steadfast presence that you are in my life.

Chapter One

We are the Source's first children—the architects of creation itself. Some of us, like me, have been exiled to this insignificant planet since the first human took their first breath.

If you haven't read the first five books, you have no idea what lies ahead. If you have, you might think you understand our histories, our powers, and the ways we've shaped human civilization. But let me assure you: you don't. Our story runs far deeper, tangled with truths you've yet to uncover.

For one thing, I blame Lilith for everything.

Whatever happened between her and Adam on this cursed earth—whatever cruelty or betrayal she suffered—changed her in ways none of us could foresee. And that change spread like a ripple across our lives, binding us to this place in ways I never wanted. Before her trauma, Earth meant nothing to me. I had no desire to leave our home. But Aryalis asked me to join her, and I couldn't refuse. Aryalis followed her mate Virgilian here; he was too preoccupied, too attuned to Lilith's anguish to ignore what he had seen in her. And then there was Soren—always Soren—who followed me like a shadow, never far from where I am, my mate since inception. So here we are, tangled in Lilith's web, stranded on this forsaken planet because she couldn't handle her own suffering. One tiny fracture in her perfect road, one taste of human pain, and she shattered. And when she broke, she dragged us all down with her.

But that wasn't enough for her, was it? She decided to go further. She thought it would be wise to insert us into humanity, to plant the essence of a yahudiyah into a mortal womb, allowing us to live human lives.

She of all people should have known better. She should have known what human suffering would do to us.

Soren, especially. Soren, the father of all tricks, the bringer of harmless mayhem. Before, his pranks were never more than harmless mischief—fun, light-hearted, a distraction from eternity. But after his first human life… something changed. That was when I saw violence in him for the first time. Real, brutal violence. Something dark had taken root in him, something he couldn't just laugh off. And it all traces back to Lilith and her foolish idea, her reckless, obsession with improving the human form.

I blame her. For all of it.

And if you want the truth, it started long before we ever set foot on this planet. It started back home, before any of this mess with Lilith.

Back in our own realm, where creation was pure potential, some of the Yahudiyah felt an instinctive pull to build. After the moment of inception, they drifted naturally toward science—the crafting of stars, the mapping of galaxies, the engineering of planets to cradle life. But not all of us shared that urge. Some of us felt different desires, subtler yearnings.

For me, it was always sound. The hum of energy, the rhythm of cosmic vibrations reverberating through the void. I didn't care about stars or solar systems. I wanted to capture the raw frequencies of existence, to shape them into intricate patterns, to create art from sound itself. My entire being thrummed with the urge to experiment, to weave vibrations into new, complex harmonies. That was my gift—my calling.

Aryalis understood. Her talents went even further; she could conduct symphonies from clouds and rain, from lightning dancing across the sky. Her storms weren't just weather; they were music—great, crashing movements of thunder and wind, delicate notes of raindrops and mist. When we combined her storms with my patterned vibrations, we created something so beautiful it defied description. Together, we could make the new universe sing.

We could have been the winners, Aryalis and I. The competition back home, the grand exhibitions of creation where the most gifted of us showcased our talents. Had Aryalis shared my ambition, we would have entered as a team. Together, we could have outshone Sarah Francis and Lilith. If Aryalis and I had dared, we could have been chosen to partner with Adam. Maybe then none of this would have happened. Maybe then we wouldn't be trapped here, shackled to a planet.

Because I would have handled it—the trauma, the pain of mortality, whatever cruelty Adam inflicted on Lilith. I would have withstood it and emerged whole. I certainly wouldn't have crumbled at the first taste of suffering, dragging everyone I cared about down with me.

Instead, here we are. All of us, stranded on this tiny, dirty ball of rock hurtling around its sun, enduring millennia of exile for her foolishness.

She returned to us altered in ways no one had ever witnessed before. Her energy, once steady and serene, now throbbed in shades of pink—bright, raw, and restless. It pulsed erratically, contracting and expanding in response to everything around her, as though each molecule in her space was an affront that she could neither ignore nor embrace. Her energy could not find stillness, ceaselessly swirling within her, an endless, vibrating spiral.

For yahudiyah, rest may not involve sleep as it does for you humans, but it's still essential. And Lilith couldn't rest. Not at home, not among us. I saw her agitation, and I chose to ignore it, hoping it would subside. Surely it would pass, I told myself. Yet the notion of her returning to Earth was not something I anticipated.

When she finally made the decision, And the others followed, Aryalis and I found ourselves amongst the others who decided to follow her. We viewed the journey through the cosmos as a rare opportunity to practice our ensemble. As we glided through the vastness of space, our energies intertwined and played against each other, sending radiant harmonics across the stars. I remember being slightly disappointed at the way my vibrations contracted in the cold of deep space, reducing my usual vibrancy to a muted hum. Aryalis, however, was still pleased; her scarlet mist undulating in sync with our movements.

All the way to Earth, we performed for the others who traveled with us, unaware that it would be the last time we'd drift so freely through the stars for millennia.

When we reached the edge of Earth's domain, something shifted. The invisible wall closed behind us the moment we crossed its boundary—a barrier unseen but unmistakably felt. The very air around us seemed to grow heavy, dense with an unfamiliar weight. Panic flared through our ranks as the realization set in: we were trapped, locked out of the cosmos with no way back.

It was here, at the boundary that marked our exile, that Aryalis made her stand. Her scarlet light flared defiantly, a radiant protest against this sudden imprisonment. "I'm not going any further," she declared, her voice a resonant pulse that echoed in the emptiness.

For a fleeting moment, I was tempted to remain by her side. Virgilian, her mate, did not hesitate. "I will stay with her," he announced, his sapphire energy wrapping around hers like a protective shield.

The rest of us lingered, reluctant to leave them behind, feeling the weight of the decision pressing down on us. Eventually, we murmured our goodbyes and continued our descent, leaving Aryalis and Virgilian alone at the edge of eternity.

I often wonder how different things might have been if I had chosen to stay by her side—or, more profoundly, if I had never chosen to come here at all. If I had resisted, Soren would never have dragged me from our realm for this reckless excursion, and he might never have tasted the temptation of human life. These days, my mind is a relentless theater of what ifs, my thoughts drifting endlessly through the possibilities of what could have been.

What if Soren hadn't found such twisted joy in setting Cain against Abel, using brotherhood as a tool for chaos? Would the pain of their endings have lessened? And what if we could have spared Seth's wife and child from the sorrow that befell them—could we have prevented the ripples of suffering that followed? Sometimes, I wonder if I should have stood with Paisley against Lilith when they bred the Samrus and Adam's children together.

I've stayed neutral on so many matters, even when I felt strongly about them. I convinced myself that standing apart would somehow balance Soren's deeds, negating his cruelty with my silence. Yet in my attempt to avoid conflict, I may have simply enabled his path. Now, I find myself questioning whether my neutrality was a form of cowardice, a convenient way to avoid responsibility for what has unfolded. The choices I didn't make haunt me just as much as those I did.
When Cain killed Abel, Eve's grief was a bottomless well, an agony that threatened to consume her entirely. She was certain that Cain had been touched by darkness from the very start, that his nature had always been somehow twisted. She and Adam had agreed their sons didn't need to know the truth—but deep down, Eve knew Cain was not truly hers.

Eve had been shaped by the Source in a single day, crafted by the divine. When she awoke, she was met with an already-grown mate and a child by her side, believing that this was simply how families came into being. But as she confided in me, she revealed something more: Lilith had visited her shortly after Eves creation, when Cain was still a tiny, fragile babe. It was just after Eve had lain with Adam for the first time, and the pain of that union was still fresh in her mind and body.

Lilith came to her in that vulnerable moment, enveloping her in her essence. She soothed Eve's pain, drawing it from her until only comfort remained. In that moment, Lilith also showed her a pleasure Eve had never known, guiding her gently to the first climax she had ever experienced. When Eve awoke to find Adam mounting her again, she found herself empowered by what Lilith had shared, and she taught him how to bring her to that same pleasure. But despite these fleeting moments of shared connection, there was something deeper that Eve felt Lilith had left behind—a shadow that lingered.

Months later, when Eve endured the bewildering, miraculous pain of giving birth to Abel—her first true child—she looked at him and saw herself and Adam reflected in his tiny, perfect form. Then her gaze shifted to the small bed where her other young son sat quietly watching. In that moment, an ancient instinct stirred within her, an intuition as old as creation itself. Cain was not truly hers.

She would tell me that she saw it in his eyes—something unmistakable, something other. They held the subtle yet undeniable resemblance to the human form Lilith had taken since her return to earth. Cain was Lilith's child, forced upon Eve by the Source, and Eve had known this truth from the very beginning, though she had never spoken it aloud.

I took those memories from her mind, leaving her free to mourn both sons as if they had each been born of her flesh. Cain was exiled from his family, unable to remain among those he had wronged. He took only his wife and children, walking a thousand miles to carve out a new life. Some of the Yahudiyah followed him, helping him establish a fresh beginning in an unfamiliar land.

Unbeknownst to Eve, I had given her a gift she didn't realize she needed. In her grief, she mourned Abel, her beloved son, but also Cain—the son who was never truly hers.

But now, looking back, I ask myself: what if I had made a different choice? What if I hadn't concealed Cain's origins, hadn't left Eve to wrestle with her grief in ignorance? Would we have allowed ourselves to live as humans, knowing that Lilith, in her madness, had not only crossed the threshold of human existence but had borne a child and abandoned him to fate?

Would Soren, Lilith, and I have walked a different path, had I not chosen silence in that moment? The questions churn within me—an endless tide of possibilities, haunting me with every unspoken truth.

This is a prime example of my own interference with human history—a moment that might have turned out differently had I made another choice. I will admit it was thousands of years before I even entertained the idea of taking responsibility for my actions. Even now, I'm not entirely certain I have truly examined the choices I made, or questioned if they were anything more than the inherent tools given to me at my creation.

It's difficult to describe what it feels like to have a mate from the moment of your existence, a bond so profound that it transcends comprehension. From that first instant, I have never known what it means to be alone. Soren has been my constant companion—a partner in every adventure, a witness to every misstep, an accomplice in every endeavor I've dared to imagine. Across billions of years, through countless planets, species, and galaxies, he has been there, an unwavering presence by my side. I never considered that this would change, nor did I ever want it to.

Soren is not merely someone I have “tolerated.” No, he is my mate in every sense, a connection I have cherished at every turn, in every conceivable way. We have shared failures and triumphs, watched civilizations rise and crumble, and woven our own mark through the fabric of existence. I don’t know if I would be who I am without him. His presence has been a gift beyond measure—a grounding force, a joy I have celebrated in ways that words could scarcely capture.

That is the Soren I need you to understand—the mate who knew every hidden corner of the land, who sought out new caves just so I could test how my voice echoed within them, each new chamber shaping my song in ways neither of us could predict. He was the one who wandered the cliffs and ravines, collecting strange, jagged stones and impossibly smooth river rocks, bringing them back to me with that spark in his gaze, as if he’d uncovered treasures. Together, we shaped the first drums, the rhythms pulsing through the earth beneath our feet.

And it was Soren who handed me a hollowed branch, its insides already worn smooth by time and flowing water—a gift from nature he'd found just for me. I remember the weight of it in my hands, light yet filled with possibility. With that branch, I carved my first flute, coaxing music from it as if breathing life into something ancient and sacred. I've kept it safe all these years, a memory of the beginning, a memory of him. The creature you see now, this so-called "monster"—this is not the Soren who has stood by my side for eons. The change in him began here, on this strange, stagnant world. Why would the Source, in its wisdom, pin someone like him to one place for so long? Soren was never meant to linger. He needs to roam, to weave his tricks across new worlds, where fresh eyes can fall for his mischief. Before Earth, we were wanderers, drifting from planet to planet, galaxy to galaxy. I would seek out new resonances, sculpting sounds in ways no one had ever heard, while Soren found endless amusement in his harmless pranks on the locals.

We were more than welcome wherever we went. Invitations poured in from Yahudiyah, from distant constellations, urging us to visit some new world, some uncharted expanse. Soren and I were like celestial travelers, embraced by councils of elders, mystics, scholars, curious to see what we would do next. Our presence was not only tolerated; it was celebrated. And we moved through those circles as equals, laughter and music in our wake. We were harmless. We were fun.

It was the confinement that had twisted his actions, dulled his humor, and sharpened his cruelty. I was certain that when the wall finally opened and we were free to leave this dreary world, the old Soren would return, piece by piece. It might take time—change always did—but he would come back to me. That was my role as his mate: to wait out the storms, endure his… hobbies, and defend him as fiercely as he defended me. That was the gift given to us, long ago, to stand by each other through all things, no matter the shape they took.

True, he'd become particularly vile here, but I found it hard to blame him. These humans were a simple species, scurrying through their lives with barely a thought beyond survival. They multiplied like insects, filling every crack and crevice of their world. If Soren killed one in a fit of irritation or boredom—well, I couldn't bring myself to mourn. Another would be born somewhere to take its place, the cycle as mindless and inevitable as weeds pushing up through stone. I didn't condone his cruelty, but nor did I feel for these humans. They were hardly worth feeling for.

Most of them were hardly worth feeling for, these fleeting, fragile creatures. But I had my favorites. I learned the hard way, though, to keep them hidden from Soren. His delight in stirring up chaos extended to me as much as anyone else, and after his first human life, his jealousy was a force to be reckoned with. Soren allowed himself countless indulgences, but he had no tolerance for mine. So if I chose to care for a human, I had to be careful—it had to be someone Soren would find utterly unthreatening, or else I had to guard it as a complete and total secret.

That was easier when he'd confined himself to a human form, as he sometimes did for reasons I never entirely understood. During those times, when he was bound to flesh and distracted by human desires, I could slip away and love as freely as I dared. And I loved deeply, without reserve, even though I knew each bond was temporary. I'll share some of those stories with you in these pages, but first, you need to understand this: all I ever wanted was to go home with my mate, to take Soren away from this world before it changed him beyond recognition. Given the choice, I would have spirited him far from here and never looked back.

At first, it was all a joke to him. When humans started calling him Satan, he laughed, reveling in the fear and fascination they held for him. When they named him Prince of Darkness, I watched as the bright scarlet of his energy deepened, darkening to a shade like old blood, a color that never faded back to what it once was. Each legend, each whispered myth, fed something in him—a desire to embody the role they'd cast him in. With every new tale, Soren's ego grew sharper, more brittle, and so did his hunger to live up to the monster they imagined him to be.

I would like to say I was oblivious to Soren's changes, but in truth, I was consumed by my own evolution. Earth was unlike any world I had encountered, a place rich with sensations I had never imagined. Here, I discovered something entirely new to me: the evolution of music.

In the beginning, it was only raw vibrations—simple, primal sounds that I could coax from the world around me, from the hum of wind through trees, the rhythmic crash of waves, or the low, resonant growl of distant thunder. Humans responded instinctively, humming along in loose, formless tunes, their voices blending with the natural world. These sounds were unrefined, but they held a strange power, as if Earth itself was singing through them.

Then, they began to shape these sounds, weaving words into the vibrations, turning noise into song. They started to tell stories through melody, layering emotion and meaning over each note. It was as if each song was a piece of themselves, a memory captured in sound. Their voices grew bolder, the songs more complex, and I found myself mesmerized by this new art form, this music that was unlike anything I'd heard in the far reaches of the galaxy.

In the worlds I knew, music was fleeting—a melody was born, lived, and died, rarely repeated. But here on Earth, a single song could echo across centuries. I watched as humans preserved their songs, passing them from one generation to the next, each version growing richer, more layered. They added instruments, sounds that hadn't existed before: strings that could weep or sing, drums that echoed like thunder, flutes that whispered like the wind. Each new voice deepened the song, transformed it, until a simple tune became a living symphony, something ancient and yet always new.

And I was at the center of it all. The need to create consumed me, driving me to invent new instruments, new vessels for sound, each one unlocking more ways for humans—and for myself—to express the vast spectrum of our emotions. I crafted hollowed gourds that sang when struck, delicate strings that quivered at the lightest touch, wind-horns that could echo through valleys. Every day, I discovered new ways to shape vibrations, bending them to my will until they seemed almost alive.

I was so intoxicated by the journey, so mesmerized by the possibilities, that I let everything else fade into the background. Soren's growing darkness, his cruelty—it became easy to overlook. My own moments of indulgence, my lapses into arrogance and apathy, seemed minor in comparison to the marvels I was creating. I told myself that as long as we were stranded on this primitive world, we might as well enjoy ourselves, immerse ourselves in what it had to offer.

And yes, sometimes that enjoyment came at a cost. A human life here, a ruined village there—trivial sacrifices, I told myself, in the grand scheme of things. After all, we were the Source's first children, the original sparks of creation. If a few lives were lost in our pursuit of beauty and pleasure, wasn't that a small price to pay? In my arrogance, I allowed myself to believe that we were entitled to this indulgence, that we deserved to shape this world in whatever way brought us joy. And so I turned away from the darkness growing in Soren, dismissing it as just another part of the game.

But sometimes, late at night, when the music finally faded and silence settled over the world, I felt the faintest prickle of unease—a shadow of doubt, easily smothered by the lure of the next creation. And so the cycle continued, my hands busy crafting new sounds, my energy blind to the cost.

So I'm going to tell you my version of the events that led us to the moment we finally broke free of this rock. Judge me however you like—I'm long gone from your planet, and your opinion means nothing to me. But if you're going to understand what really happened, you should know this: I watched Soren break away from himself the moment we crossed the wall. I know he sent a message to someone on Earth before we left. I also saw that message return so I know it was received. To who, or why? I don't know. And now that he's no longer my problem, I don't particularly care.

Seraphina and Leopold stayed behind, and Lilith… well, she let herself fall away before we even reached the wall. I watched the barrier dissolve as we passed through, so I know it can be crossed freely now. I imagine the three of them won't linger here long—at least, I hope not. Whatever kept us bound to that place is gone, and I wish them the same freedom I've claimed for myself.

But as for me and Soren? Our paths have finally diverged. I don't know what awaits us when we return home, or if it will feel like home after all this time. But I do know one thing with a strange and certain clarity: I'm done being his mate. That role, that bond, whatever it was—we left it behind on Earth. I no longer need him to define me. I'm capable of existing alone, and for the first time in eons, I want to.

There's an odd peace in that thought, a quiet certainty. It's a kind of freedom I hadn't dared to imagine when we first arrived, back when I thought we'd leave this world unchanged. But Earth has a way of transforming everything it touches, doesn't it? Even those of us who believed ourselves above its reach.

□

Chapter Two

When Lilith and Tomas shattered the landmass and set the continents adrift, a profound shift rippled across the world. The yahudiyah, our kind, saw it as an urgent call to scatter ourselves across the fractured earth, embedding within each land to observe and subtly guide the humans. The purpose was clear: to watch over their fledgling societies, to be witnesses, and at times, silent architects of their fate.

I found myself indifferent. Humanity's trivial pursuits were not my concern, and I held little desire to meddle in their growth beyond ensuring their harmonic resonance—vibrations, the music of their souls, was the only aspect worth my notice. Soren, however, was less aloof. His fascination with their unpredictability and fierce ambition drew us to Europe.

In the early years, we spent countless hours as we always had, exploring the myriad ways vibrations could be crafted to suit my needs and devising novel, spine-chilling methods to unsettle the local humans. This was a time when Soren's thirst for direct violence had not yet surfaced; instead, he reveled in the subtle art of puppeteering, steering the wills of men who held power. Hundreds of his handpicked marionettes existed before the ink of history stained parchment, and since then, hundreds more have danced to his commands. One of the earliest figures in your recorded chronicles to bear the dark mark of Soren's influence was Nero Claudius Caesar Augustus Germanicus—the infamous Roman Emperor.

Soren had singled him out when the boy was still toddling about the marbled halls of Domus Tiberiana, his infant laughter echoing among the echoic pillars and silken curtains. The child was both captivating and flexible, and Soren shaped him with a sculptor's precision, embedding whispered promises and fears deep into his subconscious. As the years wore on, those whispers transformed into a force that led Nero to a tyrant's crown, and history's tales recount his legacy in ashes and blood. The Great Fire of Rome in 64 AD, which some claim was his doing, remains shrouded in mystery. The glow of the flames reflected in Nero's dark, glassy eyes—a city burning as he strummed his lyre, absorbed in the music that drowned out the shrieks. His relentless persecution of the Christians, coupled with his opulent feasts and palatial indulgences, carved his name into stone as one of ancient times most reviled rulers.

Soren, confident in the monster he had molded, found himself intoxicated with success. He wanted more than mere influence; he craved the mortal experience in the empire he had engineered. Eager and careless, he found a suitable young woman on a scorching afternoon in the market square. The sun glistened off the mosaics of the forum, casting golden hues across the bustling crowds. Her hair shone like polished chestnut, bound neatly beneath an embroidered veil, and her robes were woven with the delicate threads that only the wealthy could afford. She was, unbeknownst to her, ripe with potential. Soren needed no second glance. He slipped through the fabric of existence, becoming a sliver of essence that wound its way into the unguarded egg nestled within her. No inquiry into her lineage or family situation crossed his mind; he assumed her luxurious attire marked her as a noble.

But assumptions are treacherous. As the months crawled on and the world around her softened with the coming of winter, the girl returned to her homeland—Enns, a bustling trade outpost in what would become Austria. Her father, a prosperous merchant, had merely been conducting business in Rome. I watched them depart, the frost of early November biting at their travel cloaks, while Soren's future grew uncertain within her womb.

I, on the other hand, preferred meticulous planning. After days of observing the townsfolk of Enns, I chose my vessel with care—a woman of modest yet comfortable means, married for years but still without a child to cradle. The townspeople murmured that the gods had withheld their blessing, but I knew better. Her eggs were fertile, gleaming with health, and the fault likely lay with her husband. It mattered little; they were devoted to each other and eager for a child. Unlike the scandal that would shadow Soren's young, unmarried mother, my arrival would be met with nothing but joy and relief—a gift from above to a couple who had nearly resigned themselves to the quiet ache of an empty household.

As the biting winds swept down from the Alps and frosted the rooftops of Enns, I nestled into my chosen mother's warmth.

Warmth. That was the first human sensation I ever knew. As a yahudiyah, the distinctions between hot, cold, or warm were trivial, abstract concepts that never penetrated our spiritual forms. Temperature was meaningless without flesh to register it. But in those earliest moments of my human existence, nestled in the dark, silken cradle of my mother's womb, warmth enveloped me like a cocoon, pressing against my forming skin and seeping into the marrow of my tiny, burgeoning bones.

I kept my presence a secret from my future mother, resisting the urge to send her soothing thoughts or whispers of my awareness. I believed that silence would ensure her peace, her body undisturbed by the unsettling notion of an intelligent being already inhabiting her unborn child. Perhaps that was my error. Despite the tales spun by other yahudiyah, recounting the profound connection and emotional symphony between mother and child, I felt none of it during that first human experience. There were no shared dreams, no melodic heartbeat that spoke only to me, no whispers of love echoing in our joined blood. I was an uninvited guest, isolated within the very core of her being.

After the initial, comforting warmth, my senses sharpened. The mild, gentle heat soon grew to a smothering swelter, a tight, confining weight pressing on every inch of me. My human body, still fragile and raw with newness, began its relentless demands. Hunger throbbed like a drumbeat, constant and gnawing, and I quickly learned that contentment was fleeting. I shifted, searching for ease, only to discover that my first flails of movement unsettled both of us. Her heartbeat would quicken with my smallest kicks, the rush of her blood surrounding me like a storm. It took weeks to realize that such movements made the space even more cramped, each twitch or stretch turning the once-gentle heat into a stifling, unbearable embrace.

Learning to control my limbs was an exercise in both frustration and revelation, a feat of will that would never be repeated in my later experiences. There, confined in the snug, dark womb, I became acutely aware of my limitations—the helpless floundering, the aches of a body not yet attuned to my will. The tales from the others who had inhabited human mothers spoke of bliss, of connection, of love seeping through the blood. But in that first, unnerving experience, the only truths I knew were warmth, hunger, and the stinging loneliness that lay beneath it all.
I channeled my energy, urging my embryonic form to accelerate its growth, weaving together sinew, bone, and flesh with a precision that defied natural human development. By the sixth month of her pregnancy, my mother, wide-eyed with both exhaustion and awe, delivered me—a child far stronger and healthier than any newborn the midwives had ever encountered. The whispers spread like wildfire through the village, marveled at during market days and whispered about over evening fires. How could a babe born so early, they wondered, emerge with such vigor and vitality?

What drew the most attention, however, was not just my uncanny strength but the uncanny resemblance I bore to my mother. Strands of striking red hair framed my tiny face, the color so rich it caught the light like woven copper. When my eyes fluttered open, they revealed irises so deep a brown they bordered on black—echoes of her own watchful gaze. The village women, bending over me as I lay swaddled, cooed and gasped. "The very image of her," they would say, shaking their heads, whether in awe or something more superstitious, I could never tell.

And they were right. That vibrant hair has become a motif in the human forms I've chosen through the centuries, a small nod to my first mother and the fire she carried within her. Even now, when I fashion myself from the ether and don a mortal guise, I often find my reflection staring back with locks of red and eyes that hold shadows of distant memories.

She named me Claudia, after her mother, saying it was in that moment she first glimpsed the hair that marked me as hers. Though I carried a sense of loneliness during my time in the womb, it vanished the instant I was cradled in her arms, replaced by warmth that spoke only of her boundless love. Choosing them as my parents had been the right decision; from the moment I entered their lives, their affection enveloped me completely. Those early years were unlike anything I had ever known, filled with joy that defied comparison.

Ours was a small town that suddenly found itself home to two peculiar infants. Soren and I were born on the same day but on opposite ends of that modest place. We were alert, more aware and capable than newborns had any right to be. It was clear that neither of us knew how to play the part of a typical newborn, and it showed in our every movement and gesture. My parents faced challenges they couldn't have anticipated, yet they embraced them with unwavering hearts. They defended their strange daughter at every turn and loved me with a fierce, unyielding devotion.

The first time the two mothers decided to place the peculiar infants together on the same woven blanket, the entire town seemed to pause as if the square itself held its breath. The market stalls, bustling with the tang of ripe olives and the low hum of trading voices, grew silent. Eyes widened in the light of the midday sun, glancing from gossiping merchants to weathered grandmothers who clutched at their shawls in awe. Even the stray dog that often roamed the square sat back on its haunches, watching with a tilt of its ragged head.

Soren and I, barely old enough to comprehend the world beyond the warmth of that shared wool blanket, turned our tiny heads in unison and met each other's gaze. A smile curved our lips, as if we were privy to an ancient joke the onlookers would never understand. To the townspeople, it was a sign—two souls destined to be entwined. But to us, it was proof that our plan had worked.

I knew this would succeed, Soren's thought slipped effortlessly into my mind, his infant eyes bright with mischief.

You knew nothing, I projected back, my own smile daring him to argue. You don't even realize that we are no longer in Rome! I had to trail after you, miles from the empire you were so fond of, and convince fate to place me in this small, nameless town.

Soren's gaze flickered, almost imperceptibly, but then he shrugged, a feat that was more mental than physical in our tiny forms. It matters not, he responded, dismissing the distance and the disarray of our reincarnation. What's important is that we're here, and we will grow up together.

His calm confidence had always both irritated and comforted me. He spoke as if the moment were already wrapped in inevitability, a future spun tightly in fate's loom.

When we revisited this conversation years later, Soren confessed that the months spent growing inside his mother's womb had been the most wondrous, almost divine experience of his existence. He said he had communicated with her, a soft and ancient whisper in her mind, urging her to find a husband swiftly, before any rumors could sprout. And she had. She married a blacksmith who worked for her father. He had a shy smile and hands blackened by the forge, and for that, Soren felt secure in the warmth of her love long before his first breath.

Their bond, he told me, felt as though it spanned millennia, as if he had inhabited her dreams for a thousand years. And when the time came for his name, he had toyed with her through fragments of visions, dreams of marble columns and the grand echoes of imperial halls. Eventually, she spoke the name aloud—Nero—inspired by the stories she'd heard of a beloved emperor, and he had cooed, a sign of agreement.

Our childhood in the sleepy town of Enns was almost idyllic, painted in hues of sun-dappled meadows and the rhythmic clanging of the blacksmith's forge. Although Soren's mother had married a blacksmith, his grandfather was the wealthiest man in town, the lord of a sprawling estate that towered above the surrounding rooftops. The house, built from stout stone and crowned with ivy-laced gables, seemed almost as old as the town itself. Its windows like watchful eyes, taking in the laughter of grandchildren that spilled across the wide cobblestone courtyard.

Unlike my quiet, reserved home, where the walls whispered more than they sang, Soren's house was a constant flurry of voices. His mother was one of four lively daughters and three strapping sons, and they brought with them an entourage of children and grandchildren. The place teemed with life—young cousins darting between rooms, the scent of bread baking in vast ovens, and bursts of laughter that resonated like music in the open hallways. Soren, with his mischievous smile and easy charm, thrived in that chaos. He had an uncanny talent for blending in, mimicking the common cadences and gestures of townsfolk with effortless grace. And when we were together, he passed on his little tricks: how to tilt a head in conversation to seem genuinely intrigued, the perfect pause before a laugh, the subtle nods that made others feel heard.

In contrast, I was often told I walked and spoke like someone older, a soul trapped in the careful steps and deliberate words of the past. My parents were quiet scholars, and I had spent countless hours under their watchful eyes, absorbing their debates about philosophy and history until it seeped into my very mannerisms. Where Soren could slip in and out of roles as easily as changing a cloak, I was always scrutinizing, always observing. But somehow, he found delight in this and in me, and he made it his mission to pull me into the light of his boundless world.

The grand house on the outskirts of town became a sanctuary for me, a place where I was invited to shed the burden of being an observer and become a participant. Its great halls, adorned with tapestries that depicted the town's storied past, felt like a second home. I can still remember the feel of the worn wooden floors beneath my feet, the mingled scent of smoke from the forge and wildflowers from the garden drifting in through open windows.

From a very young age, my gift became a marvel to my parents and the townspeople. Any instrument placed in my hands—no matter how complex or unfamiliar—sang as though I'd known it my entire life. What they couldn't have known was that I once stood among those who first helped humans craft these very instruments. Mastering them now was mere child's play.
By the time I reached ten years old, I could command a whole ensemble's worth of instruments. My fingers plucked melodies from the lyre, delicate and reverent, perfect for hymns or quiet gatherings. The cithara, with its deeper, richer voice, made crowds stop and listen, whether in festivals or public squares. When I cradled a lute, rarer in our town, its strings resonated with whispers of ancient tales. Even the primitive harps would yield mournful or joyous songs depending on my whim.

But as word of my talent spread, Soren's grandfather grew restless. "The emperor must see this!" he muttered, eyes glinting with a dangerous mix of pride and ambition. It was then that I noticed an unfamiliar flicker in Soren's gaze—jealousy, a shadow that had never graced the eyes of a yahudiyah before.

We were beings of pure essence, capable of love, anger, humor, and sadness—emotions that formed the spectrum of our existence. Yet stepping into human vessels changed us in ways we hadn't anticipated. The rush of blood, the surge of hormones—these added layers, complex and often unsettling, triggered new feelings. We hadn't known these borrowed emotions would linger, shaping us even after we left the flesh behind. And there it was, jealousy, seeping into Soren's heart and shifting something fundamental between us.

I managed to stay composed, convincing myself that his reaction was only born of concern. After all, these bodies were fragile, newly formed and untested by long journeys or the whims of powerful men. Soren's protective nature, I reasoned, masked itself with envy.

Facing his grandfather, I softened my features and spoke with practiced meekness. "I have no desire to play for anyone outside this room," I said, embodying the role of the shy village girl whose dreams stretched no farther than her town's borders and the comfort of a good man's company.

It was a performance, one I hoped would buy us time before ambition and envy could tip the balance of our fragile human lives.
I let it be. To venture into the emperor's courts now would be folly, especially with the fragility of our human disguise. For both our sakes, the world beyond the town would have to wait.

And then, one evening when the sun dipped low and turned the sky into a canvas of red and gold, we became more than just companions. The first time we made love, it was in the quiet sanctuary of the upper room, where the beams creaked as if sharing our secret. His eyes, always so full of mischief and warmth, turned serious, and in those moments, I felt something more than just the rush of youthful passion. I felt the ancient bond between us solidify, cementing my fate as surely as stone set in mortar.

It was then that I knew: whatever time was allotted to me on this earth, it would be marked by him—by the shared laughter, the whispered dreams, and the unspoken promises that wove us together more tightly than any vow.

We married not long after, as if it had been written in the stars. The whole town expected it; from the day we were born, whispers of destiny followed us like a shadow. No one batted an eye when, barely more than children, we exchanged vows beneath the open sky, the scent of wild rosemary drifting through the warm summer air. Our early years were golden, marked by laughter that echoed in the narrow, sun-drenched streets and the shared conviction that we had all the time in the world. Onlookers predicted we would follow in my parents' footsteps, choosing to start a family later, when life was more settled.

Soren thrived under his grandfather's tutelage, working tirelessly as an apprentice turned partner in their merchant trade. He was sharp-eyed and quick-tongued, famous for striking deals that left even seasoned traders marveling. His grandfather, once stooped with worry over the future, now stood taller, pockets heavy with coin and pride. I devoted myself to our household and the women of our community, offering help and companionship. I played my instruments in moments of joy and sorrow, their familiar notes weaving into the fabric of our small town's life, but always within the intimacy of family gatherings or town festivals.

Then came the whispers, faint at first but growing louder—the murmur of war moving like a shadow across the neighboring valleys. Soren, ever confident, decided to act. "They need to see reason," he told me one night, fingers tracing idle patterns on the wooden table between us. "If I speak to the general, perhaps we can avoid bloodshed."

He left at dawn, the sky tinged with hues of lavender and orange, a ancient being in the body of a boy. The Roman camp loomed large and imposing, tents lined in neat, disciplined rows, the metallic clank of armor a constant undercurrent. The general, broad-shouldered and disinterested, met Soren in a tent rich with the scent of spiced wine and oil lamps that flickered against the heavy fabric. He watched with a predator's eyes as Soren spoke of loyalty, alliances, and the emperor’s distant glories he spoke of the emperor as his namesake. The general’s face was carved into an inscrutable mask, but his gaze shifted briefly, a silent signal.

Back in town, the first cries tore through the morning stillness—sharp, raw, and terrified. By the grace of the Source, I was visiting my parents that day. My father’s hands, usually so gentle and steady, trembled as he guided my mother and me into the cramped crawlspace beneath the floorboards. The air down there was thick and stifling, but it couldn’t muffle the chaos above.

Through the narrow cracks, I watched boots hammer across the dirt floor, raising clouds of dust that hung in the pale light. The sounds followed—doors splintering beneath brutal blows, screams that began in terror and ended too abruptly, and the sickening metallic rasp of swords slicing through flesh. Each noise struck like a hammer to my chest, reverberating with helplessness and dread.

Soren's mother and her sisters had no such hiding place. The soldiers, brutal and relentless, ravaged them while the men who were still alive were forced to watch, eyes wide with horror and helpless rage. When their cruelty was done, they executed them all, leaving bodies to cool under the indifferent sun.

Soren returned just as the soldiers began wiping their blades clean, their faces smeared with sweat and the satisfaction of easy conquest. Something ancient flared in his eyes, a fury too deep for human expression. He moved then, not like the trader's son they knew, but like a seasoned warrior possessed by divine wrath. His body, impossibly fast and precise, twisted and struck with a strength that defied explanation. Each Roman he met fell with a look of bewildered shock, blood pooling dark and silent beneath them.

The last soldier gurgled out a warning, eyes bulging before Soren silenced him with a clean, brutal sweep of his blade. Breathless and covered in their blood, he stood amidst the bodies, a figure transformed. Not even the whispering wind dared to break the silence that followed.

That's where he stood when I found him, among the wreckage and the bodies, his eyes fixed on something far away, something only he could see. The person I had loved was gone. In his place stood a beast, forged in blood and grief, who knew nothing of limits or mercy. His transformation was complete that day, and I watched as the ember of cruelty within him fanned into an inferno.

In the years that followed, Soren channeled every ounce of himself into securing our town and defending his family's estate He enforced a relentless state of readiness; weapons were sharpened at all hours, and watchtowers rose like sentinels over the outskirts. But readiness alone could not heal the scar of loss, nor could it satisfy Soren's hunger to reclaim what had been taken from him.

One evening, with the weight of shadows thick between us, he turned to me and spoke words I never thought I would hear. "I must produce my own children," he said, voice flat as if stating an indisputable fact. But I could not give him what he wanted. So he sought it elsewhere, driven by a cold, unyielding logic.

He took young, frightened girls plucked from the countryside, their faces blurring together in my memory. He left his seed scattered across the land, indifferent to the fate of those who carried it. I lost count as the years rolled by, but the whispers spoke of hundreds of children born, half-blooded remnants of a legacy built on desperation. Yet even this did not sate him. He nurtured a festering hatred for the Romans, provoking skirmishes, testing their patience, daring them to return.

And return they did.

This time, Soren was prepared. He moved with a ruthless precision, long before the Roman columns darkened the horizon. His eyes met mine as the first war cries shattered the dawn; they burned with a familiar, consuming fire. He said. “You’ll see. I will kill them all.”

I believed him. I wanted to believe him. So I stayed, fingers curling into the folds of my dress, listening to the clash of metal, the shouts, the sudden silences that swallowed men whole. But his plan unraveled as the Romans surged, wave after relentless wave. His small band of fighters, no match for the trained legions, fell like wheat under the scythe.

The house trembled as the Romans broke through. Soren and I were cornered, just the two of us in a room that now felt unbearably small. His eyes met mine, not with the fear or regret I expected, but with a hardened resolve. “They won’t take you,” he whispered, voice steady as stone. And then he lunged, hands finding my throat, crushing the air from my lungs.

The world dimmed, pain arcing through me like lightning, until darkness swept over everything. That was how my first human life ended—at the hands of the man I loved.

But death was not the end for me. My true form, raw and unbound, surged forth in a blaze of fury. I expanded, ethereal limbs stretching out as wide as the house, slicing through the walls, the invading soldiers, everything in my path. Their screams were brief, cut off as I swept through them, a storm of vengeful essence. I flowed through the town, taking out every Roman within a ten-mile radius, leaving only silence and the dark stain of vengeance behind.

I expected Soren to rise then, to shed his mortal shell and join me as we once were—free, beyond the reach of human frailty. I hovered, waiting for the shimmer of his essence. But he did not come.

For twenty more years, Soren lived as a man. He remarried, fathered legitimate children, and rebuilt a life that, in its way, honored what had once been ours. And in that space, I became his vengeance. His revenge was mine to carry out, and carry it out I did, with all the fury that two lifetimes could muster.

Soren's thirst for retribution had called to me. The Romans' treachery had long festered in his heart, and their reach—unchecked had spread to a tipping point. It was time. I descended upon the city like a storm born of rage and ancient power, invisible and unstoppable. I swept through the grand halls where marble statues of Roman gods looked on, their cold eyes betraying neither judgment nor pity. The crackle of flames followed in my wake, at first a whisper, then a roar as fire licked at wooden beams and silk draperies, turning them to cinders.

When I found Nero, draped in robes too fine for the monster beneath them, he was lounging, eyes glazed with wine and indulgence. He didn't even have time to scream. I surrounded him, my essence coalescing into a scorching, ethereal blaze. His body contorted, twisted by agony as I seared him with the heat of a thousand suns, his skin blistering and splitting under the force of it. He was reduced to nothing more than charred bone and ashes, a wisp of smoke where an emperor had once reclined.

But I wasn't done. Vengeance needed a face, a memory to etch itself into the minds of those who would tell this story for generations to come. My form shifted, energy reshaping into his likeness. I stood tall in the heart of his palace, lyre in hand, strumming a haunting, discordant tune as the fire consumed everything around me. The flames painted the sky crimson, their tongues leaping up as if trying to touch the heavens. I played, eyes hollow and staring out over the chaos, while the city screamed—a symphony of panic and crackling timber, of collapsing stone and distant wails.

The heat singed the very air, wrapping around me as if trying to reclaim its maker, but I played on. Let them say it was Nero who watched with cold detachment as Rome burned. Let them believe he plucked his lyre while his people perished. The truth didn't matter; only the legend would remain. And in that legend, my vengeance would be eternal.

□

Chapter Three

When I recounted to Soren every sordid detail of Rome's fall—the flames devouring marble and stone, the shrieks of the panicked masses echoing through the narrow streets, and the sight of Nero reduced to a husk—his joy was palpable. It radiated from him, a triumphant, almost manic light that set his eyes ablaze and pulled a rare smile to his hardened face. In that fragile moment, when he was unguarded in his happiness, I made my request.

"I want to be born again," I whispered, the words slipping out as if they were alive, as if they had been waiting for this precise instant. His eyes clouded, the war between logic and longing playing out in the brief furrow of his brow. But he nodded, against his better judgment.

The choice sealed, I entered the young wife he had taken—barely more than a girl, with wide, fearful eyes and a body that trembled under the weight of expectation. She carried me as an unseen, silent force, my essence entwining with her lifeblood, settling into the space meant for human thought. Yahudiyah energy does not share the mind; it claims it entirely. We take root along the spinal cord, thread through veins and arteries, until we command the form from the inside out.
This time, I chose to craft myself differently. I shaped the body with deliberation, softening my essence and molding it into a boy. It was I consider a great deal before settling on my choice. When I was born, Soren's expression was masked under a flicker of surprise that edged into something darker.

As I grew, his unease festered. It was there in the tightness of his jaw when I laughed, in the way his eyes narrowed when I reached out to touch an instrument or ran barefoot through the fields, hair catching the sunlight like a net of spun gold. Eight years passed, each one heavy with a silence that buzzed between us like a swarm of wasps.

Until one day, the silence broke.

It came in a rage as sudden as a storm, with words spat like venom and hands that seized me before I could flinch. His eyes, once familiar, were now wide and alien, pupils blown with something that went beyond hatred. He shouted, but I couldn't grasp the meaning over the ringing in my ears and the pressure closing around my throat. The world spun in a dizzying blur of colors as darkness clawed at the edges of my vision. And then, just as before, my human life ended at the hands of Soren.

But it didn't stop there.

I felt my essence, disoriented and raw, hovering in that liminal space between flesh and freedom. I sensed him, a predator with shaking hands and shallow breath, violating the shell that had once housed me. It was an act of power, a futile attempt to reclaim control, to smother whatever it was in me that terrified him. His betrayal seared into the energy of my being, etching a new, cruel truth: Soren, the man I loved.

When he was done, his chest heaved with each labored breath, and he turned to me, eyes hollowed by a strange mixture of relief and guilt. “I cannot bear seeing you as a masculine,” he said, voice trembling but resolute. “It is unnatural. You are free to be as you like, but not that—not in my sight.”

His words sank into the silence between us, jagged and cold. My essence pulsed with the weight of his declaration, disbelief mingling with a fury that surged hot and ancient. He had stripped me of the form I had chosen, replaced acceptance with judgment. The air around us crackled as I drew closer, wrapping my energy around him, not tenderly as I had done so many times before, but like the tightening coils of a serpent.

His eyes widened, a flicker of recognition flashing across them—he knew what was coming, and yet he did not move. I felt him shudder as my essence constricted, pouring into him, smothering the life from his frail body. He crumpled to the ground, a marionette whose strings had been violently cut.

As his spirit left the confines of its mortal shell, it expanded in a burst of scarlet light, stretching itself across the sky, luminous and immense. It was as if I had not murdered him but had freed him from a cage that he had outgrown. His presence filled the town, pressing against my awareness like an endless ocean.

He looked at me, no trace of anger marring his form. Instead, there was an almost playful glint in his spectral gaze. "Now we're even," he said, his voice carrying both laughter and melancholy, echoing in a place where sound had no right to be.

He had killed me when I was only eight, confused and full of life. And I had killed him as a man, burdened by years and sins. But there was no satisfaction in this balancing of scales, no peace in the symmetry of our deaths. Only the hollow realization that the cycle had completed itself and left us both diminished.

Soren had changed, shedding the remnants of who he once was like a snake outgrowing its skin. Now, with newfound resolve burning like molten iron within him, he saw his path clearly. Outside the fragile confines of his human form, his potential for destruction was limitless, and he was ready to wield it with a calculated ferocity. The next hundred years would be marked by a single, unyielding purpose: forging men into ruthless instruments of war, bred to annihilate anything that bore the mark of Rome. His ambitions stretched far beyond mere skirmishes; he envisioned campaigns that would rend the land itself, reducing Roman cities to smoldering ash and echoing the cries of a crumbling empire.

The first instrument of his wrath would be Boudica, the indomitable Queen of the Iceni. She was fierce, her eyes blazing with the fire of a leader scorned. Soren saw her as more than just a warrior—she was the spark he needed, a weapon crafted by injustice and sharpened by pain. Once, the Romans had flogged her, violating not just her body but her spirit, stealing what could never be returned. They underestimated the power of her vengeance, and Soren would ensure that this mistake would be their undoing.

Boudica's legacy was already formidable. To the Britons, she was a lioness, fierce and unyielding, a symbol of defiance against the iron grip of Roman rule. To the Romans, she was a nightmare made flesh, a villain whose rebellion left their proud empire reeling. Soren envisioned the columns of black smoke rising from Londinium, the embers swirling like ghostly fireflies, and he knew it would only be the beginning. The devastation she wrought had already scarred the empire, and under his shadowed influence, it would bleed deeper.

He wielded an unseen influence, sowing seeds of destruction both within and beyond Rome’s formidable walls. Inside the city, he corrupted powerful men, stoking their ambitions and darkest desires until they set the stage for chaos. Men like Caligula, the infamous Roman Emperor, were prime instruments of his machinations. Caligula’s reign, brief yet marked by unprecedented cruelty, saw the empire's treasury drained by his extravagant pursuits and twisted spectacles. His mercurial behavior bordered on madness; he declared himself a living god, demanding worship and slaughtering those who questioned his divine right. With every act of tyranny, Caligula fractured Rome's stability, setting loose a storm of fear and mistrust that weakened the empire from within.

Beyond the city, he whispered into the ears of those who stood in the shadow of Rome's might, turning their eyes toward conquest. His voice reached men like Hannibal Barca, the Carthaginian General, who became a relentless specter haunting the Roman Republic. Hannibal, renowned for his military genius, rallied his troops with the promise of Roman blood, crossing the towering, snow-laden Alps with an army bolstered by war elephants—a feat so audacious it became legend. His strategic brilliance brought Rome to its knees on multiple occasions, devastating its forces and threatening its very survival.

It was during this era that my passion for channeling my energy into instruments to be wielded by the finest musicians first took root. While Soren laid siege to Rome, I roamed freely, untethered by time or place. Whenever I encountered a musician whose talent met my high standards, I would become their instrument—my essence woven into strings, keys, or pipes, awaiting their touch. The music we created together resonated beyond mortal limits, each note ringing out with an intensity that surpassed any sound their earthly instruments could ever achieve.

This was the first time I felt the stirrings of true affection for a human. His name was Ambrose, later known as Bishop of Milan, a man whose voice and touch could conjure divine melodies from the air. Together, we wove harmonies so beautiful that they seemed to ripple through the very fabric of time. The music we created came to be known as the Ambrosian chant, an ancient form of plainchant that paved the way for the more structured Gregorian chants. Even now, the echoes of our creations linger in the stone walls of cathedrals and the solemn breaths of choristers. Ambrose had a presence that drew me in—a luminous blend of wisdom and insatiable curiosity. When we played together, time melted away, leaving only the pure, unyielding ecstasy of creation. I took on countless forms for him: the resonant curve of a lute, the deep-chested warmth of a wooden lyre, even the fragile grace of an aulos. He wielded each one with a mastery that made my spirit tremble; it was as though he could feel the thrum of my essence beneath the strings, beneath the polished wood and bone.

In one such moment, overcome by the sheer delight of our union, I let my guard slip. The music soared around us, spiraling higher, and before I knew it, I revealed the truth of my being. I spoke of the Yahudiyah, the ancient and hidden, those whose existence ebbs and flows like wind, unseen but ever-present. I watched as understanding flickered in his eyes, a mixture of awe and the faintest shadow of fear.

But our joy knew no bounds, and I continued to shift and morph, presenting myself as dulcimers, flutes, and harp strings strung tight and quivering under his nimble fingers. Each transformation was a silent declaration, a bond deepened through the language of music.

We were so entwined, so intoxicated by the fervor of creation, that I did not notice Soren, watchful, lurking in the shadows of the porch. His presence was a cold weight, distant yet unavoidable. I will never know what passed between Ambrose and Soren, what silent warnings or unsaid words. What I do know is that one day, as I assumed the form of a harp ready for Ambrose's touch, he did not come. Days stretched into months, and the air felt emptier without him.

I searched, extending my senses to the far reaches of cities and countryside alike, but he was gone—swallowed by a fate Soren would never divulge. The music we shared became a ghostly echo, haunting my thoughts. In the ache of loss, I learned the cruel lesson of vigilance and restraint. I learned that love, even when draped in harmonies and strung across the span of instruments, must be guarded fiercely.

Next, I chose another human life, though, like Soren, my choice of parentage was less than ideal. My cries were the first thing to disturb the silence of dawn as I was discovered swaddled on the frostbitten steps of the Sisters of Saint Helena. The stone façade of the nunnery, cold and unforgiving as the people within, became my home—a place where piety was wielded like a whip. I was raised under the strict gaze of Mother Anselma, her prayers more like curses hurled at the devil she insisted lurked in every shadow I cast. Every whispered prayer was a reminder that this was not my place, not my life.

By the time I was fourteen, the simmering resentment that coiled in my chest ignited into a blaze. My voice, which had never carried weight beyond murmured hymns, roared Soren's name into the night. His response was swift, shadow slicing through the candle-lit hallways. Silence fell, heavy and final, in the wake of his unseen blades. Blood darkened the sacred stones, staining the silence that had once been so suffocatingly holy.

When the villagers arrived, led by the glint of torchlight and hushed murmurs, Soren watched, waiting like a beast in tall grass. Their eyes went wide with horror before they fell, one by one, bodies crumpling as if felled by the wrath of God himself. It became our pattern, our waltz of blood and shadow. I, the waifish girl with a smile that didn't quite meet my eyes, and Soren, a specter who exacted punishment on those too foolish to see their own doom.

There was something almost poetic in those early days of our journey. Men, emboldened by hunger or darker cravings, would stagger out from roadside and forest clearings, leering as they drew closer. I'd feign fear, the glisten of unshed tears making my eyes shine like glass. And then Soren would emerge, invisible but terrible, and I'd watch the men's smirks dissolve into screams. Their eyes bulged, muscles straining in final, useless attempts at survival. Sometimes, as their gasps rattled to silence, I'd step over them, my skirts brushing their cooling skin, and smile. It was almost delightful, knowing their final moments had been spent in the horror they'd intended for me.

And so, for a time, this became our new game. We would weave in and out of human lives, taking turns inhabiting the fragile shells of mortal bodies while the other lingered nearby, ever watchful, cloaked in shadow. Life was undeniably more thrilling when you knew an unseen protector waited in the dark, ready to rend apart anyone who dared threaten your facade. The thrill lay not only in existing as humans but in exploiting the vulnerability that came with it, turning it into a weapon against the unsuspecting.

Soren embraced his incarnations with reckless abandon, leaving behind a legacy that stretched across kingdoms. He would charm, deceive, and conquer, scattering his progeny like seeds in a windstorm—bastards with sharp eyes and tempers to match their father's. Rumors of wild-eyed warriors with a mysterious lineage began to swirl, adding to the myth of his presence, though no one could piece together the truth.

I, on the other hand, found my joy in performance. Music became my weapon of choice, and my delicate fingers danced across strings and keys, weaving songs that left audiences spellbound. No town or city could resist my allure; I became the virtuoso with the haunting melodies, the slight, beautiful girl who captivated crowds under the glow of lanterns. Yet in my wake, stories crept through alleyways and whispered in market stalls—tales of the grisly fate that followed those foolish enough to covet or harm the girl who could master sound.

They never suspected me. How could they? I was always too slight, too ethereal, with eyes that sparkled like stolen starlight and a laugh that was all mirth and innocence. But behind that mask, I was already seeking my next stage, my next audience to dazzle and deceive. And if a hand lingered too long on my waist or a glance grew too hungry, Soren would shift from shadow to retribution, silent but deadly. I could almost taste the terror in their last breaths, a bittersweet reminder of how fragile life was when you were human—and how easily we could snuff it out.

When not in human form or standing vigil to protect me, Soren worked tirelessly, a shadow on the periphery of history, engineering the slow, inevitable downfall of Rome. His soul, forged in grief and vengeance, had been set ablaze by the loss of the only mother he had ever loved although he had man others, taken by the very empire that he now sought to destroy. Each move he made was as calculated as the strokes of a master sculptor, chiseling away at Rome's power until it was but a cracked and weathered relic of its former grandeur.

Soren infiltrated the minds of Rome's leaders, sowing seeds of greed and ambition that bore poisonous fruit. He whispered in their ears during the darkest hours of the night, urging them to push for heavier taxation, to drain the last coin from the people's purses. Inflation spiraled, warping the value of currency until trade faltered and poverty spread like a plague. Slave labor became a crutch, an unsustainable pillar that held up a crumbling economy. Resources dwindled, hoarded in the estates of the elite, while the empire's coffers echoed with emptiness. Rome's financial mismanagement festered under his subtle prodding, like an untreated wound on the body of the empire.

To Rome's enemies, he was a ghost, a fleeting whisper in the smoke of their campfires. He shared visions of glory, fanning their hunger for conquest. Under his invisible guidance, barbarian tribes such as the Visigoths and Vandals united and struck with sharpened purpose. Soren watched, satisfied, as the Visigoths stormed through the city gates, their blades reflecting the fire-lit horror on the faces of those who once believed themselves invincible.

But Soren's schemes did not end with battle cries. He laced rumors among the people, whispers that grew into shouts in the streets, of the corruption that ate at the heart of Rome's leadership. Senators with hands slick from bribes, emperors who rose and fell with the predictability of a gambling game—Soren ensured that their instability fractured trust. Civil wars erupted like storms, breaking the empire's unity until its very identity began to splinter.

He played the rich like puppets on gilded strings, tempting them into decadence. He taught them to turn a blind eye to the needs of the state, to gorge themselves on opulence and excess. The sheer weight of the empire's size, its borders stretching thin and vulnerable, became an Achilles' heel. Governors and generals, distracted by power struggles and the comforts of luxury, allowed Rome's once-impervious walls to rot from within.

Even culture itself was not spared Soren's insidious touch. He coaxed civic pride to falter, stoking an atmosphere of detachment and indulgence. Gladiatorial games became more brutal, the cheers of the crowd more bloodthirsty, as if the very soul of Rome craved its own self-destruction. Public life shifted from noble duty to reckless pursuit of pleasure. The social fabric, once vibrant and unbreakable, frayed into strands too weak to hold.

And so, he watched as Germanic tribes and the ferocious Huns prowled the borders, emboldened by the scent of Rome's decay. He guided their steps, invisible hands urging them to push where the walls were weakest, where the guards were complacent. Each raid, each broken battlement, each night of screams and chaos was another verse in the requiem of Rome, composed by Soren's tireless orchestration.

Rome's collapse was no accident, nor was it the result of fate alone. It was the work of a shadow, a grief-stricken being who had dedicated centuries to the ruin of those who had taken what he held most dear. And when the final stones of Rome's great monuments crumbled into dust, Soren stood unseen, listening to the silence that followed—his vengeance finally complete. Years later, he would smile at the final act: the Ostrogoth King Odoacer's triumph, when Rome's last emperor was dethroned, signaling the death knell of an era.

When Rome finally fell, I thought that would be the end of our insatiable thirst for power, at least for a while. The sight of smoldering marble, the acrid tang of smoke in the air, and the chorus of despair that echoed through the ruins should have been enough to quell our desire. For once, I wanted peace. I suggested we find a hidden cavern somewhere in the northern expanse of the Americas, a place where human voices were but a distant murmur and the landscape hummed with untouched beauty. There, the auroras would drape themselves like shimmering curtains across the sky, their colors shifting in spectral dances. The acoustics of the stone halls would catch the whispers of the wind, mingling them with the low thrum of the earth's core, a perfect harmony to soothe my restless spirit. I imagined Soren and I there, enveloped in silence, the echoes of our shared past dissolving into the embrace of nature.

But Soren, with energy that still glinted with the wild gleam of conquest, would not listen. He was drunk on the triumph that came from reducing an empire to ashes, drunk on the knowledge that every stone toppled was a testament to his will. Rome was not just a city to him; it was a canvas for his power, and now it lay broken, its proud columns snapped and its streets littered with the debris of fallen gods. He craved more. Africa, he declared, was next.

The continent pulsed with life, a vibrant mosaic of kingdoms and clans, guided by the deft hands of Virgilian, Leopold, and Seraphina. Cities sparkled with gold-tipped minarets and marble marketplaces; the voices of traders and scholars blended in a symphony of dialects that told stories of centuries past. Yahudiyah here now chided him, their laughter lilting like the chime of ceremonial bells. What once had been admiration for the architect of Rome now transformed into sly mockery, a reminder of his disaster. They sent their emissaries, scholars from the Moorish lands, across the Mediterranean to teach the Europeans the basics of literacy and hygiene, their rich, melodic language a balm over centuries of barbarism.

Soren could not bear it. The humiliation settled in him like molten lead. His energy clenched as he recalled how we had been left to guide Europe, and how our stewardship had brought only stagnation and folly. So, he resolved that we would embark on our familiar cycle—his life reborn in human form, then mine, unfurling across the expanse of Africa. It was a dance we knew well.

While Soren reveled in the thrill of dominion, I sought the music that lay hidden in the pulse of the land. I infused my human incarnations with the magic of sound: the deep, resonant calls of my drum that mimicked heartbeats; the nimble strings of the kora that sang of rainstorms and sunlit mornings; and the wistful flute, whose notes carried the voices of ancestors across time. I made music the spine of every story, every celebration, weaving it into the identity of the people so it would outlast even us. It was my way of finding beauty amidst Soren's relentless ambition.

But Soren’s conquests took a darker turn. He walked among the kingdoms with an insatiable hunger, eyes blazing as he claimed women for himself, leaving the seeds of chaos in his wake. The traditions he seeded grew twisted: rites that spoke not of unity but of power plays and dominance, rituals that splintered families and strained the bonds of tribes. Where I gave song, he offered strife, weaving cycles of upheaval into the fabric of generations.

Everywhere we traveled during those days, Africa was a tapestry of immense diversity, marked by powerful empires, bustling trade networks, and profound cultural and technological progress. Yet Soren, with his insatiable thirst for chaos, sowed seeds of cruelty and greed that tainted even the brightest of times. In the bustling trade hubs of the Swahili Coast, where merchants from Arabia and India exchanged goods, he whispered deceit that turned alliances into rivalries. In the majestic Ghana Empire, a land of gold and prosperity that controlled the trans-Saharan trade routes, Soren's influence festered, convincing leaders that conquest was the only path to dominion.

As the Aksumite Kingdom struggled under the weight of its decline, its proud Christian heritage under threat, Soren manipulated faith into fanaticism, setting brother against brother. He moved like a shadow among the expanding Bantu-speaking peoples, using their dispersal to spread discord, urging one tribe to see another as an enemy, promising power to those who yielded to his poisonous words.

Soren's most insidious machination came when he fed into the minds of men a singular idea: that they should hold dominion, and women, the keepers of life and harmony, should cower beneath their command. His influence reshaped societies, hardening the hearts of those in power and silencing voices that once called for balance and respect. His whispers reached across the sands to reshaped the lives of countless women, who were thrust into a reality where their voices would not ring with equality again for thousands of years.

Soren thrived in the chaos of conflict, and wherever he went, human turned on human, convinced that strength lay only in dominion and division. The dynamic landscape of Africa—a continent of growth and profound change—was also a stage where Soren played his dark symphony, weaving his influence into the ambitions and beliefs of all who would listen.

There was an insatiable urge within Soren to hunt and kill the Yahudiyah whenever they inhabited human form, an impulse so deeply rooted that it bordered on obsession. He relished every opportunity to end their lives, savoring the dark satisfaction it brought him regardless of the era or the place. The thrill drove him to take great risks, and more than once, he sacrificed his own mortal existence just to claim one of their lives.

Virgilian, Leopold, Seraphina, and the others knew that no corner of the world was safe from Soren's relentless pursuit. They learned to move in shadows, hiding their mortal lives behind false names and concealed existences. But even the most careful deceptions and remote refuges were not enough to protect them. Soren's twisted sense of victory peaked one fateful night when he found Leopold and Seraphina. It was their wedding night, a rare moment of joy and unity, and perhaps the only reason Seraphina had allowed herself to remain in human form. Soren shattered that night, plunging it into blood and horror, ending both lives before they could even consummate their bond.

That murder marked a turning point. The survivors had suffered enough. In a rare alliance born of shared grief and fury, Virgilian and Leopold bound themselves in a powerful act of sacrifice, creating a makeshift prison of their combined energies. They trapped Soren in a construct so forceful that it anchored him to a single place, immobilized for months. It was a feat thought impossible until then, an act that defied everything known about our kind. Despite my every attempt to reason with them and suggest alternatives, they refused to release him.

Soren's entrapment became a standoff, each side holding its breath as the months turned over like restless tides. Only after Soren, his pride fraying under confinement, swore an oath to leave Africa and never return did Virgilian and Leopold relent. They dismantled the prison with a reluctant finality, the unspoken understanding that such a truce came at a steep cost—a fragile peace balanced on the edge of betrayal.

□

Chapter Four

We returned to Europe, a land steeped in stories and song, where I dove deeper into an unexpected passion—a deep, resonant love for blending poetry with music. It was as though the very vibrations of the world called out to me, each note pulsing with untold verses. One night, casting off the bounds of my human form, I drifted as a wisp of ethereal energy, seeking a vessel to embody my inspiration. I found it in the slender, ink-stained hands of a young boy, a peasant whose dreams were humble and whose heart was pure. Through him, I scribbled feverishly by candlelight as if possessed by the muses themselves. His quill darted across the parchment, conjuring verses that paid homage to the great epics—the heroic deeds of Beowulf and The Song of Roland, tales once recited to the strumming of strings and the haunting notes of flutes, passed down to preserve the spirit of a bygone age.

This nocturnal ritual became my secret devotion. I claimed the hands of peasants and the voices of wandering bards, infusing the land with new tales, new harmonies. Soon, the Early Middle Ages gave way to an era richer still—the High Middle Ages. It was during this time that the cacophony of single melodies grew more intricate, blossoming into the majestic complexity of polyphony, where multiple, independent voices wove together like the threads of a vibrant tapestry. In these centuries, I thrived, my influence flowing like an undercurrent beneath the surface of mortal creation. For reasons I did not yet understand, these were the years when my creative force surged without pause or hindrance, allowed to unfurl and echo across courtly halls and quiet village squares alike.

Soren did not interfere with my activities for what seemed like an eternity. The question of his whereabouts and the purpose of his ventures never crossed my mind, content as I was in my realm of poetry and the vibrations that carried my art through the ages. His visits became part of a rhythm I had come to accept—fleeting but frequent enough that I always knew all was well. He would appear with a smirk or a silent nod, a signal that he was about to embark on yet another of his enigmatic adventures. Then, just as quickly as he came, he would vanish, leaving me to my verses and the hum of melodies that thrummed in the air like whispered secrets.

This became our pattern, a wordless understanding that endured for thousands of years. I never strayed far from Enns, the place where we first lived our human lives, where the river's song was as familiar as our own breath. It anchored me, and even as I shifted between forms—human or otherwise—he could always find me with ease. Soren needed only to cast out his mind and call; the thread that connected us was unwavering, and I would respond without hesitation.

As for what he did during his long absences, I knew little and asked even less. When he felt particularly triumphant, he would regale me with tales of his exploits—stories woven with chaos and glee. Yet, these moments were rare, and rarer still was my inclination to probe. The unspoken truth between us was that we each thrived in our chosen realms: mine steeped in creative silence and the haunting beauty of poetry, his in the relentless pursuit of whatever stirred his dark, insatiable spirit.

When Europeans began venturing to the Americas in waves, I saw it as an opportunity to explore uncharted territory and experiment with new experiences. Driven by curiosity, I too crossed the vast ocean to witness the world unfolding on the other side. I found myself reborn into a modest town nestled in the northern reaches of this new land, a settlement where settlers struggled to carve out a life amidst untamed wilderness. My family, recent arrivals with hopeful eyes and hardened hands, sought to make a home, clinging to their beliefs as if they were lifeboats in an unknown sea.

The native people, generous and resilient, tried earnestly to teach them the ways of their land: how to hunt, plant, and live in harmony with the cycles of nature. But their wisdom clashed sharply with the rigid doctrines of the settlers' faith, and whispers of heresy curled through the narrow roads like smoke. I, spoke to them as a mere girl with wild ideas and attempted to explain the true origins of their faith—what Virgilian had intended when he first shaped their beliefs. But my words were met with outrage and fear. The townspeople, seeing my insights as blasphemy, condemned me and handed me over to the natives as if I were a burden to be cast away.

Rage coursed through me, hot and unyielding, and I called for Soren. He answered swiftly, a storm in yahudiyah form, eyes glinting with the promise of ruin. In moments, the village emptied as if it had never been, its people vanished into nothingness, leaving behind silence more deafening than any shout. Yet, Soren's wrath did not stop there. He unleashed his fury upon the bewildered natives, who had done no wrong but stand witness to this nightmare. Despite my protests, he swept through them, scattering their souls like autumn leaves and, with chilling precision, destroyed the fragile human body that housed me.

"You are not for this place," he said, voice low and edged with finality. "Return to Europe. Return to your instruments, your verses."

I sensed that he was right; this part of the world was not yet ready for beings like us. But even as he prepared to lead me back across the sea, I heard the deep, resonant beats of the native drums. Their music reached me, raw and primal. I knew that my influence had already seeped into the rhythm of this new land long before I got here, Without another word, I let Soren guide me back to Europe.

I have stayed here, bound to this world, for what feels like an eternity. To be truthful, I have found myself engaged in peculiar acts, even by the standards I have long upheld. I have witnessed the intangible turned into something tangible—vibrations transcribed, given permanence on scrolls, and brought back to life in repetition. It is a marvel unique to earth, a testament to the audacious creativity of humankind. In the vast expanse of the universe, music holds little significance, reduced to a fleeting shimmer of sound without consequence. But here, on Earth, music is everything, a force woven deeply into the fabric of existence.

I often ask myself, is this profound connection a product of our confinement? Has our long stay on this spinning sphere, far longer than any other, birthed this boundless devotion to sound and meaning? On other worlds, I bring vibrations—the raw essence of creation itself—and offer them to the chosen species. They receive these gifts, twist them into forms that suit their needs, crafting rudimentary expressions that mimic the intention, but fall short of the intricate dance that humans have mastered. Nowhere else do vibrations evolve into what they become here: symphonies of sound, words imbued with emotion, stories that resonate across generations.

Unlike any other, humans have harnessed these creations, preserving them in physical forms that defy the ephemeral nature of sound. First came the rough carvings on vinyl records, then the whispered secrets stored on magnetic tapes, the crystalline echoes of CDs, and now, the invisible data of digital recordings—capturing every nuance, every breath of music, and archiving it beyond time. Such feats are unheard of, unmatched across the cosmic expanse. Only Earth can claim this legacy, and I am sure it is the result of my influence.

Had I been granted the luxury of millennia with another species, especially those whose intellects surpass even human capacity, we might have forged similar paths. We might have etched music into the heart of other worlds, bound their histories to melodies and rhythms. But I was never anchored to any place for long, drifting instead from one civilization to another, a wanderer with only fleeting time. Here, however, my roots dug deep, and my impact has pushed the boundaries of what music can be. Now, at last, I stand on the cusp of sharing this wonder with the universe, eager to bring forth a gift born solely of Earth's improbable genius.

This is what I have waited for, the culmination of my endless yearning. It is all I desire now—a chance to touch the farthest reaches of the galaxies with the music born of Earth. While that moment still lies beyond my grasp, I have found solace in the pursuit of patience, immersing myself in its subtle, often excruciating art. Patience is not just the quiet act of waiting; it is the discipline of stillness, the embrace of dormancy that reaches beyond mere inaction. I have spent lifetimes perfecting this, allowing myself to become the silent companion of renowned musicians, a vessel for their genius, lying dormant for decades at a time.

I have learned to embody art itself, not merely to create it. Soren and the others speak of me in hushed tones, in awe of my ability to remain utterly motionless, a sculpture of potential energy, without a glimmer of movement for decades. They cannot fathom the restraint, the way I hold myself as if I am stone, the way I refuse even the slightest tremor until summoned. And then, only when a master approaches—one whose hands have been sculpted by years of devotion and precision—do I allow myself to awaken. In those moments, I surrender to their touch, springing to life as a living resonance. My form shudders, vibrates, and sings in ways that reach into the soul, creating sounds they never dared to imagine.

To those who witness it, this sudden transformation is a revelation. To me, it is the fulfillment of my purpose, an act that threads together centuries of silent practice with fleeting moments of transcendent harmony. And when the final note fades and silence reclaims the air, I return to stillness, a sentinel awaiting the next touch worthy of awakening. This is how I prepare, how I hone my gift, until the day I can unfurl it across the cosmos, weaving Earth's music into the very fabric of the universe itself.

And although I rarely question Soren about his activities, the evidence of his descent into a cruelty I had never imagined became impossible to ignore. It began with whispers of suffering that grew into wails, spreading plagues across continents with a swiftness that defied reason. Epidemics that should have burned out in months instead devoured entire populations within days, leaving streets littered with the lifeless, their silence more deafening than any lament. The scale was staggering, more destruction than I ever thought possible, and yet, it was only the beginning.

His reach extended into the hearts of men, fanning the flames of conflict until they raged out of control. His manipulations turned the Holy Wars from battles of faith into blood-soaked orgies of power and carnage, events so savage that even I, who had long resigned myself to human folly, had to intervene. I begged him, pleaded for moderation, asking him to find less ruinous ways to amuse himself. For a time, he heeded me, but it was merely a pause in his relentless pursuit of chaos.

The transatlantic slave trade soon became his latest fixation, a grotesque spectacle that fascinated him for decades. I remember one particular argument with him, when he boasted to King Leopold that he could sow suffering without ever stepping foot on African soil. And he proved it, his influence turning human greed and prejudice into an unstoppable tide that swept millions into the hold of ships, bound for lives of agony and toil.

Then came the birth of a new horror, one that made even the most hardened souls shudder—his bastards, as I came to call them. Across the globe, they began to emerge: individuals who took pleasure in killing, not for power or necessity, but for the sheer ecstasy of it. They were the first serial killers, and through them, Soren's madness rippled through society, darkening the human experience in ways no one had seen before.

But even this was just a prelude to what came next. His devices pushed the world into an era of unparalleled violence. It was Soren’s hand I sensed in the rise of tyrants, his shadow behind the events that led to the cataclysms of the First and Second World Wars. When the horrors of war gave birth to industrialized killing, when the camps rose with their black plumes of smoke reaching to the indifferent sky, I refused to share in the guilt. Soren's delight was laid bare when he confessed to influencing Heinrich Himmler, feeding him the dark visions that turned the Holocaust from a concept into a monstrous reality. I had accused him of living too much in the moment, of having no regard for the long-term consequences of his whims. His response was a bitter smile and words that chilled me: “You wanted me to find focus, and I did.”

But even as his name became synonymous with fear and death, he seemed bewildered by my horror, unable to comprehend why I was not impressed by the magnitude of his creation.

As always, even in the midst of unspeakable horrors, there were moments of light. Fleeting and fragile, these moments were like threads of gold woven into a tapestry of shadow. Between the chaos, we lived human lives—brief, incandescent existences where we shared the profound bond that only intimacy could create. Soren understood the power of such connections, the way that the act of intercourse bound us together in ways that transcended mere companionship. Every few centuries, he would orchestrate these mortal interludes, slipping us into human forms and casting us into lives where we could experience love, desire, and the raw vulnerability that came with them.

It was in those lives, lived within the boundaries of flesh and time, that we found a fragile kind of peace. For a heartbeat in the grand symphony of eternity, we were not beings of influence and manipulation but simply lovers, tasting the sweetness of what it meant to be mortal. Our shared laughter, whispered secrets under the canopy of stars, and the silent moments spent entwined in the dark were powerful enough to soothe the discord between us. In those moments, I could almost forget the monstrous acts, the orchestrated tragedies that Soren reveled in when the veil of humanity was lifted from us once more.

But I was never blind to his motives. I knew that these lifetimes were as much manipulation as they were genuine, that he used them to tether me to his side. He understood that no force, no demonstration of power, could bind me as tightly as shared touch and the echoes of human love. Knowing this did not stop me from surrendering to it each time. The lure of those brief moments of connection, the illusion of a simpler existence, was irresistible. They were the balm that soothed the deep, jagged wounds his cruelties left behind.

And so, I allowed it, even welcomed it, knowing full well that these human interludes were not just acts of love but calculated respites in our otherwise tumultuous eternity. They were the shimmering beads strung along the dark thread of our existence, moments where we were not gods or monsters but simply two beings who craved each other's touch. It was that longing, that fragile connection, that kept me at his side despite the storms of blood and fire that he conjured. Each time, I told myself it was different, that perhaps this time, he might change. But deep down, I knew the truth: these were just stolen moments, bright sparks in an eternal night, designed to keep me bound to him, and I allowed it willingly.

Eventually, I took on the guise of Mozart's piano, a silent witness to genius. Though I never met him in the flesh, I watched from a careful distance, captivated by the boy whose fingers danced across the keys with a precocious brilliance that seemed almost supernatural. I stayed on the periphery of his life, suppressing the yearning to be closer, to share in the electric current of his genius. Deep down, I knew that if I showed even a flicker of the interest that simmered within me, Soren's attention would shift as well, and he would not allow young Mozart to become the towering figure the world needed him to be. The shadow of Soren's influence was too great a risk. So, I kept my distance, sacrificing my desire to witness his talent up close so that humanity could have his music in its entirety, untainted by us. I surrendered myself to being his prize piano only after his death.

The same restraint kept me from Beethoven, the brooding virtuoso who thundered out symphonies as if wrestling with the divine itself. His life was marked by tragedy, each blow shaping him into a figure of mythic proportions. Yet, for all the calamity that sculpted his journey, I can say with confidence that neither Soren nor I had a hand in it. Beethoven's struggles were his own, a testament to human resilience rather than our meddling. I took solace in the fact that for once, the music of the world was born free of our entanglements, pure and raw.

But I am not without my faults. I must admit that many of the so-called members of the "27 Club," those brilliant artists who burned brightly and died too young, fell under my influence. Their raw, uninhibited talent called to me in a way I could not resist. I became a muse, an unseen presence that whispered inspiration in the quiet moments of creation, and they, ever sensitive to the pull of something greater than themselves, listened. I should have stayed away, let them flourish or falter on their own, but my longing for their artistry drew me in. And in my presence, they shone brighter, created more fervently, but often at the cost of their own survival. That guilt is mine to bear.

However, I was absent when the world lost Lennon. His death, though as shocking as a lightning bolt from a clear sky, was a result of something beyond Soren's machinations and my wandering influence. The young man who pulled the trigger was driven by something darker, something purely human and mundane in its senselessness. As far as I know, Soren did not manipulate that moment, though I can never be completely sure. The echoes of his games have reached so far and twisted through so many lives that sometimes even I can't untangle the threads. Yet in my heart, I believe Lennon's end was one of the tragedies that came solely from humanity's own hands.

In the weeks leading up to Virgilian's message, I could sense that our time on this planet was drawing to a close, like the last delicate notes of a symphony fading into silence. For the first time since the birth of creation itself, I felt a true sense of pride in what I had accomplished. My legacy was etched not in stone or flame, but in the evolution of music—a relentless, organic force that had grown beyond its primal roots into a sophisticated language that could speak to the souls of millions. It was my magnum opus, the finest work of my immortal existence, and the discipline I had gained in the art of patience was a craft worthy of admiration and study.

The anticipation of returning home, of standing among my peers and showcasing my newfound mastery, sent a thrill through me. I imagined their reactions vividly: Capricio, my male counterpart, whose playful arrogance would falter as he listened to recorded music for the first time, his gaze widening with disbelief as he realized the depth and reach of my work. And Andrew, the counterpart to Aryalis, ever the skeptic, would find himself uncharacteristically speechless. The idea of music captured, preserved, and played back at will would shatter their understanding of sound as a fleeting gift.

I pictured myself presenting the wide array of Earth's musical tapestry: the profound harmonies of Bach, the soaring intensity of Beethoven's symphonies, the rebellious flair of Chopin's nocturnes. But I would not stop there; I would take them on a journey through centuries, revealing the relentless pulse of jazz that defied convention, the raw, unfiltered cries of blues that spoke of human suffering and resilience, and the thunderous energy of rock and roll that ignited an entire generation. And finally, I would bring them to the modern age—hip-hop, a genre born from streets and struggles, whose beats and poetry had become the voice of a new era. I imagined their faces as they heard the rapid-fire lyrics, the deep, resonant bass lines, the symphony of samples and rhythms that layered together into something both chaotic and brilliant.

Capricio, who had always claimed that pure improvisation was the only true form of expression, would be silenced as he witnessed how humans had taken spontaneity and preserved it, spinning it into art that could be relived a thousand times. And Andrew, so fond of symmetry and structure, would be captivated by how human music defied those very constraints, finding new ways to express itself that defied logic yet struck at the heart.

I could not wait to unveil it all, to watch their disbelief turn to awe as they realized the heights I had reached during my millennia on Earth. The idea of sharing this, of teaching them that music was no longer a mere momentary expression but a living, breathing entity that could be captured, held, and played back at will, was exhilarating. I would finally prove that our time here had not been in vain, that my devotion and endless patience had yielded something truly worthy. It was not just the end of our stay; it was the crescendo before the curtain call, the moment where I would stand before the universe and share my greatest gift.

In the days leading up to Virgilian's message, Soren had grown uncharacteristically quiet. His usual swagger, the gleam of mischief that lit him, seemed dimmed as he spent his days lounging in the museum where I posed as Mozart's famed piano. By day, I held myself in perfect, reverent stillness, my polished surface gleaming under the soft, artificial lights. Visitors shuffled by, cameras clicking as they admired the craftsmanship, oblivious to the living presence within. I listened as tour guides recited rehearsed facts about the instrument's history, their voices a low hum that passed through me like a river over stone.

At night, when the museum closed and silence draped the room like a velvet curtain, things were different. Some nights, the staff hosted special concerts, drawing in world-famous pianists who played to enraptured audiences seated beneath grand chandeliers. It was during these performances that I allowed myself to resonate fully, ensuring that each note vibrated in perfect harmony, as if Mozart himself were whispering approval from the beyond. The air would shiver with the sound, and for a moment, I felt like I was fulfilling my truest purpose.

But on quieter nights, when the hall stood empty and the echoes of the last applause had faded, Soren and I would retreat to the shadows beneath the marble staircase. There, shielded from the silent monuments to art and history that surrounded us, we talked for hours about what awaited us after our time on Earth finally ended. His dreams were as grand as they were dark, each plan a sprawling web of conquest that stretched from one edge of the cosmos to the other. He spoke of domination, of subjugating every planet and bending its inhabitants to his will, his eyes gleaming with a dangerous light that reminded me of the old days.

I listened, sometimes amused, sometimes weary, as he wove tales of the chaos he would unleash. My ambitions were simpler, quieter. "Go ahead," I would say, a smile ghosting over my features that only he could see. "Conquer every world between here and home. I'll be waiting for you when you're done."

For a few fleeting moments, it felt like things had returned to what they once were—before Earth, before the weight of centuries and our intertwined stories of power and influence. We would laugh, voices soft as the starlight that filtered through the museum's high windows. He would lean against the cold stone wall, gaze drifting to the ceiling as if he could already see the celestial expanse he longed to reclaim. But then, as always, something would spark in his restless mind. His grin would sharpen, and before I could stop him, he'd push off the wall and disappear into the night, slipping into the world to find new mischief to orchestrate.

I would sit there alone in the echoing silence, feeling the loss of him like a shadow lengthening across me. The moments of peace were brief, fragile things that never lasted, shattered by the irresistible pull of whatever chaos called to him next.

It was on one of those restless nights, when the moon cast pale, skeletal light across the museum's polished floors, that I realized Soren was gone again. I neither knew nor cared where he had slipped off to this time. His absences were like sudden gusts of wind—unpredictable, leaving behind only a fleeting chill. I had grown used to it, accustomed to the gnawing silence he left in his wake. It was in that quiet, while I lingered in the hollow echo of his departure, that I felt the unmistakable shiver of Virgilian's message threading through the stillness.

"I have found a promising solution to our escape problems. Please come and bring the hell spawn with you. Do not delay, as time is of the essence. Expect to see everyone. Prepare yourself and control your mate. Here is my location."

The words hung heavy in the air, shimmering with urgency. Control your mate. I almost laughed at the audacity of it. Control Soren? The very thought was absurd. Since the dawn of existence, since the first breath of creation stirred the silence, Soren had been untamable. He moved like a storm, wild and consuming, bowing to nothing and no one. To even suggest I could rein him in was a fool's hope. Virgilian should have known better. Yet the message told me more than it intended. For him to call us together, to risk assembling all of us in one place, meant that whatever solution he'd uncovered had teeth. This was no idle scheme or half-formed idea. This was something real, something that could finally shatter centuries of confinement and deliver us home.

The certainty of it settled over me like an electric current. I had felt it for months, a subtle tug at the edge of my awareness, an instinct whispering that the end was near. Home was no longer just a distant dream; it was an impending reality, a song that hummed just beyond the horizon. The prospect filled me with a pulse of excitement, tinged with the bitter taste of caution. The path to freedom would not be straightforward, not with Soren's appetite for chaos at play. He would be both our greatest strength and our most dangerous liability. Keeping him in check was a task I had failed at for millennia, and now, when success teetered on a knife's edge, the stakes had never been higher.

The silence wrapped around me like a shroud, thick and expectant, as if the very air had paused to witness what would come next. My mind raced through a maze of strategies, each one a desperate attempt to keep Soren focused—to guide him without making him feel guided. Any overt control would be met with defiance, a storm I couldn't afford to unleash now. But perhaps, if I could frame Virgilian's plan as a challenge worthy of his cunning, I might steer him, if only for a moment.

I was still untangling the threads of my plan when Soren appeared, materializing from the shadows like smoke curling into shape. The look on his face was already dark, a twisted mask of irritation.

“That fool dares to try and control my actions,” Soren growled, his voice a rumble that reverberated through the museum’s vaulted ceilings. His gaze, cold and sharp, glittered with menace. “I will do as I please.”

Keeping my gaze soft, I answered with a voice that resonated like the first note struck on a grand piano, measured and calm. “Virgilian has a plan, Soren. He’s called us to that city on the East Coast of America that he’s always held in such high regard.”
Soren snorted, rolling his eyes with theatrical disdain. “Another of his tedious schemes,” he spat. “And let me guess—you’re eager to participate.”

I tilted my head slightly, my expression unyielding but serene. “He said we should expect to see everyone,” I replied, allowing the significance of that to hang between us.

His scowl deepened, a flicker of intrigue momentarily softening the edges of his anger. The idea of a gathering, of facing old allies and adversaries, sent a current of restless energy through him. I could see it: the wariness battling with excitement, the calculation behind his gaze as he imagined all the new ways to bend this reunion to his will.

"Oh, an invitation to a party?" His tone dripped with sarcasm, but the grin that followed was wicked, gleaming like the edge of a blade. "Whatever shall I wear?"

"Perhaps you could wear your best behavior, at least until we see if this grand idea has any merit," I said, a light edge of warning in my voice. Soren's smirk faltered for the briefest of moments before twisting into something more dangerous.

"And what of your precious curators?" he asked, his tone thick with mockery. "Won't they miss their prized piano when it vanishes into thin air yet again?"

A smile tugged at my lips, one laced with a touch of mischief. "Oh, they will," I replied, almost amused. "But they've become experts at wheeling out the replica they keep hidden away. It's quite the show, watching them maintain the illusion that I'm still here."

We shared a laugh, the sound rich and layered with irony. The absurdity of it all—humans, so proud of their ability to preserve history, never realizing that their most treasured relics held more secrets than they could ever fathom. I had destroyed the original of course when I decided to take it's place. Their attempts to mask my periodic disappearances were almost endearing, a testament to their stubborn refusal to accept the inexplicable.

"Every now and then, it's fun to watch them panic," I added, my tone light, smile glimmering. "They hide the truth so well, keeping their little mystery away from the public eye."

Soren's chuckle was low and dark. "It's almost too easy to toy with them," he said, his energy reflecting the thrill he found in their ignorance.

I glanced at him sideways, my expression softening. "Not everything has to be a game of terror, Soren. Sometimes it's just... amusing to let them flounder, lost in their small, safe mysteries."

"Amusing for you, perhaps," he replied, a predatory gleam sparking in his gaze. "But I prefer a touch more... chaos."

"Try not to cause too much trouble before we see what Virgilian has in store."

"Trouble?" His voice was a low growl, the sound of it reverberating through the marble floors beneath us. "Trouble is the only thing worth wearing to this so-called 'party.'"

"Try not to provoke Leopold this time," I said, a note of genuine warning in my voice. "He's still furious over the business in France. And as much as Virgilian despises what you did to Joan, you must have known she was one of Leopold's human descendants. You made a permanent enemy of them both."

Soren's grin widened with malicious delight at the mention of her. "Poor little Joan," he drawled, the French accent he mimicked dripping like venom from his tongue.

My expression hardened, darkening into an unyielding stare. "You knew exactly what you were doing, Soren."

He shrugged, unconcerned by the repercussions. "I was bored. And she was... intriguing. Her convictions, her strength—it made it all the more delicious to watch her unravel. And besides," he added, his tone turning gleeful, "it wasn't me who lit the match. Humans have always been so eager to burn what they don't understand."

My lips pressed into a thin line, the weight of ancient grievances settling between us. "Be that as it may, you crossed a line."

Soren waved dismissively, the gesture as careless as his smirk. The thought of Leopold's wrath was nothing more than an amusing trifle to him. "Leopold is a sentimental fool, too attached to his human playthings. I have no rules and Europe, And Virgilian... well, disappointment has been his closest companion for centuries.

I sighed, a weary edge to my tone. "I know staying out of trouble is impossible for you, but for my sake, try. At least until we hear what Virgilian has planned."

Soren's energy gleamed, the predatory hunger in him sharpened by the tension in the air. Leopold and Virgilian—two misguided beings trapped in their own ideals. Soren's lips curled into a twisted smile as he considered the irony. They spoke of escape, of finding their way home, but didn't they realize this world had already changed them, made them who they were now?

“Enough,” I said, shaking my head. The conversation was spiraling into futility. “It’s a long journey to the East Coast. We should go.” My voice held a note of impatience, though I kept it gentle. “I’m sure by now Virgilian has reworked his plan to account for your... unpredictability. Frankly, I’m surprised he invited you at all.”

A low, dangerous chuckle rumbled from Soren. “As am I,” he said, amusement dancing in his gaze. “But I’m just as curious as you are to see what requires my presence. Whatever it is, I have no doubt it will be... entertaining.”

“Your idea of entertainment always seems to end in disaster for everyone else,” I muttered, fighting to keep the frustration out of my voice.

Soren’s smirk widened. “That’s what makes it so entertaining.”

"Let's go then," I said, abandoning any further argument. The night fully enveloped the city, cloaking Salzburg's cobblestone streets in shadow. With a graceful sweep, I unfurled my form, letting it shimmer as it dissolved into the wind, merging seamlessly with the night.

Soren followed, his transition less elegant but charged with an intensity that left the air thrumming in his wake. He shot upward, finding a swift current of air that would carry us westward. I joined him effortlessly, our forms streaking across the sky like twin specters, unseen by the mortal world below.
Far to the west lay our destination, an American city steeped in history and mystery, a place where Virgilian's influence had taken root over centuries. The stars above blurred into a glittering river as we crossed time and distance, moving faster than any human eye could fathom.

"After all this time, to see everyone together again..." I broke the silence, my voice soft, laced with curiosity and trepidation. "This plan must have merit. Virgilian wouldn't call us all without reason."

Soren remained silent, his energy fixed on the horizon, but his vibrations told me everything I needed to know. Whatever plans Virgilian had in store, Soren was already plotting how to twist them to his advantage. The real challenge would be steering him through it long enough to see if escape was truly within our grasp.

"I'm not asking you to be anything but yourself," I said finally, my tone softening. "But if there's even a chance we can finally go home..."

Soren's response was deceptively smooth. "Of course," he said aloud. But inwardly, I knew his answer was far more ominous: Maybe.

□

Chapter Five

Traveling with Soren was always deceptively simple. He preferred to control our pace, finding pockets of wind with preternatural ease and dragging me along as if I were a leaf caught in a storm. I knew that with my abilities, we could have reached our destination much faster, but challenging Soren's fragile temper this close to Virgilian and Leopold was a risk I was not willing to take. Letting him lead was a concession I made without protest.

The house where Virgilian had arranged our meeting stood at the end of a narrow, cobbled street, tucked under the shifting shadow of the dense, silver-etched trees. It was modest but meticulously maintained, its stone walls wrapped in ivy that glistened in the moonlight. For an instant, I hesitated on the threshold, a fleeting thought to announce our arrival and avoid unnecessary confrontation flickering in my mind. I could sense the other presences inside—resting, unaware. This gathering of Yahudiyah was already a powder keg, and Soren's arrival would be the match.

But Soren had no interest in subtlety. "Conceal yourself," he instructed, his voice a low rumble that resonated like distant thunder. We cloaked our presence from detection and moved into the house between the tiny cracks in the walls. The house greeted us with an unnatural stillness, its occupants submerged in the deep breaths of sleep. Seraphina's presence vibrated softly from an upstairs room, a hint of warmth surrounded by the faint signatures of Paisley, and Leopold. But it was Sandy, Virgilian's human pet, curled up in the den, that captured Soren's attention.

The sight of the boy was unexpected. Humans were rarely involved in Yahudiyah matters, and I felt a pang of pity rise unbidden as Soren's gaze sharpened. He valued humans as one might regard a cracked mirror—fascinating only until its purpose failed. I knew what was coming.

The boy must be part of Virgilian's plan. Though Virgilian isn't here, the boy sleeps in a house full of us, Soren's voice whispered into my mind, curiosity sharpening its edges. I want to wake him.

Do not kill him, I warned, trying to make my voice sound detached, as if the boy's life didn't matter. If he's here, Virgilian has placed importance on him. Do not anger him so soon.

Something is already killing him, Soren's reply was chilling in its nonchalance.

All the more reason not to scare him to death, I shot back, my irritation mounting.

A cruel smile twisted Soren's lips, his energy gleaming with perverse amusement. I won't kill him, he promised, the words hollow and slick like oil.

His energy surged, dark and oppressive, seeping across the room in tendrils that prickled the edges of reality itself. His body contorted, limbs lengthening and bending at impossible angles, the nails at the ends of his fingers morphing into claws as his eyes gleamed like molten gold. Fangs jutted from his mouth, curved and wicked, while a low growl reverberated through the room, shaking the furniture and scattering papers like frightened birds. The beast within him relished the fear it would soon drink.

But when Sandy awoke, there was no scream, no scramble of limbs in a desperate attempt to flee. The boy's eyes fluttered open, his face caught between drowsiness and mild curiosity. He reached for the lamp beside him with a lazy hand, squinting as if Soren's monstrous form were merely a shadow he'd seen a hundred times before.

Soren's expression froze mid-snarl, confusion breaking through the feral facade. Seriously? he muttered, his mind brushing mine with irritation and disbelief. From where I stood, I watched the boy's indifference, a slow smile spreading across my lips. Sandy was slight, all angles and shadows, his wispy blonde hair sticking up at odd places, pale green eyes studying Soren with more interest than fear. Who the hell is this boy? I wondered.

Before Soren could move to tear through Sandy's defenses or seek out the terror he craved, Leopold materialized, stepping from the thin air with an elegance only a Yahudiyah could possess. He positioned himself between the human and Soren, shoulders squared, his presence a steadying force that sent an unspoken command through the room. For a moment, Soren's dark power wavered, and he considered retreat, the subtle shift in Leopold's eyes promising contact neither of them was ready to have.

Though Sandy's eyes widened and the faintest tremor flickered through his limbs, he remained composed, a startling contrast to the beast that loomed mere inches from him. His fear hummed just beneath the surface, a quiet undercurrent that never rose to the crescendo of terror Soren craved. The tension crackled in the room like a taut wire ready to snap, and I could see Soren's rage tightening around him like a vice. His dark form shifted, muscles coiling as though preparing to lunge.

But then the atmosphere shifted, a subtle but undeniable change in the energy around us. A presence brushed against the edges of my mind, familiar and foreign all at once. Before I could fully process the sensation, my gaze was drawn to the doorway. There, haloed in the dim light filtering through the cracked shutters, stood Sarah Francis. Her figure was graceful, her posture regal, and her expression unreadable. The air felt heavier, as though the house itself held its breath.

It had been so long since any of our kind had crossed the expanse between worlds. The Yahudiyah who had been trapped here with me since the dawn of man's creation had long given up hope of seeing reinforcements. And yet, here she stood—unbothered, composed, as if no time had passed at all. Sarah Francis, the first yahudiyah to make the journey to this forsaken planet since our entrapment, had arrived.

Soren's eyes narrowed, the beast within him receding slightly as curiosity tempered his rage. His claws retracted halfway, the tips of them still glinting under the fractured moonlight. "So," he drawled, a twisted grin breaking over his bestial features. "Come to see the animals in their cages, have you?" His voice was a mix of amusement and bitterness, layered with a challenge he dared her to take up.

Sarah met his gaze unflinchingly, her eyes the color of smoldering embers. There was a quiet power behind them, steady as an ancient tree. "I see no cage," she replied, her voice soft but iron-willed, each word falling like a stone in a silent pool.

"Of course you don't," I cut in smoothly, keeping my tone neutral. I wasn't sure how Soren would react to her presence, and I had no intention of finding out the hard way. "You're free to leave whenever you like, I assume?" I watched Sarah carefully, hoping my interjection might shift the tension in the room.

Her gaze flicked toward me, and a ghost of a smile curved her lips. "I haven't tested that theory yet," she said, the corners of her mouth hinting at some private amusement. "But I assume so, yes." Her voice held no tremor, and in that calmness, the simmering hostility between Soren and Leopold seemed to shrink.

I turned my attention to Soren. His monstrous form seemed to shift and waver, claws fully retracting now, though the hunger in his eyes lingered. It was as if Sarah's presence had poured water on a smoldering fire—not extinguishing it, but keeping it at bay. I glanced at Sandy, who blinked lazily, his expression almost annoyed, as if he wished we would all leave so he could go back to sleep. The sheer audacity of his calmness made me stifle a chuckle.

“Why don’t we test it out?” Soren said, a wicked light returning to him, a spark that promised mischief. His grin widened, sharp and predatory, revealing teeth that had not yet reverted to their human state. “Let’s go to the wall and see what happens.”

I glanced at Sandy again and nearly laughed at the exasperated expression that flitted across his face. His eyes, half-lidded with exhaustion, seemed to say, Yes, please, go test your theory so I can get some damn sleep. The absurdity of it all almost broke the tension, but then Sarah’s gaze shifted to Soren, and for a moment, silence wrapped around us like a shroud. Sarah Francis stood unwavering, her eyes holding Soren's wild, golden glare, “Why don’t we wait for Virgilian?” she suggested, her voice gentle yet unyielding, a tone that could silence chaos like a mother guiding an unruly child. “Then we can do all the tests you like.”

As Sarah engaged Soren with her cool logic, I couldn't tear my attention away from Sandy. The boy had not only stayed composed but had even fluffed his pillow and nestled back as if he were watching a spectacle rather than being part of one. The sheer audacity of it made my lips twitch in a suppressed smile. But Soren darkened, his gaze thinning to slits as his frustration brewed.

“I’m only here because Virgilian claims to have a way home,” Soren spat, each word sharp with resentment. “If he can deliver on that, then fine—I’ll behave. But if I’m stuck here any longer, I make no promises about my behavior.”

The room seemed to exhale, a brief lull before the storm, and I noticed Sandy’s eyelids drooping, the boy on the edge of slipping back into sleep. But the moment was shattered by a voice, smooth and dripping with theatrical charm, slicing through the tense silence. “You’ll misbehave no matter what,” the voice chimed, laced with mockery and electricity.

I turned, and there, materializing in the doorway, was a swirling mass of energy, crackling with vibrant hues of indigo and silver. The tempest solidified into the figure of a young man whose features mirrored Sandy's so perfectly that it felt as though the boy were staring at his own reflection come to life. But where Sandy was pale and calm, this doppelgänger radiated a manic vitality, eyes alight with wild intent and a wicked grin stretching across his face.

"Geminus," Soren acknowledged, his tone mingling irritation with a touch of grudging amusement.

Geminus sauntered into the room, his aura sparking like a storm ready to break. Tiny bolts of lightning snapped around him, the air charged with the scent of ozone. "I couldn't resist showing up early," he drawled, a smirk pulling at the corner of his mouth. "Ginevra's not far behind, of course. Still dragging herself around in that drab human form, so naturally, she has to rely on their clunky modes of transport." He rolled his eyes, waving a hand as if the thought itself were a tedious burden. "But I raced ahead—I had to see what all the fuss was about."

Geminus's eyes, dark and gleaming, landed on Sandy, and his smile deepened into something more sinister. "And what do I find? A delectable little mortal, practically flirting with death!" His gaze devoured Sandy, a predator's appraisal that promised delight in every reaction.

To my surprise, Sandy met Geminus's stare with a smirk of his own, defiant and bored, as if to say, You don't scare me, not one bit. The boy's audacity stirred something in me, an unexpected admiration for his fearlessness. This human, small and fragile as he was, stood unfazed before the most formidable beings in the room. I wanted to cheer for him, to commend his nerve, but I knew better than to draw Soren's attention back to the boy.

"Leave him be," Leopold commanded, stepping between Sandy and the threat once again, "He is not for you—or any of us." His tone was firm, leaving no room for argument.

Sandy, to my surprise stood up out of bed defiantly behind Leopold, peered around him with an unexpected spark of courage. "So, you're one-half of the Gemini twins," he said, his voice trembling ever so slightly but his eyes steady. "Virgilian has mentioned you." The words hung in the air, and I wondered how Leopold was going to stop Geminus from killing the boy where he stood. Not many of us enjoyed the petty nicknames. My nickname implied I should have goat horns growing out the side of my head. Why would I need goat horns and who first envisioned me that way.

Geminus's reaction was immediate and violent. His features contorted with a rage that seemed to bend the very air around him, veins bulging at his temples as if they might burst. His eyes, now blazing like trapped storms, crackled with dangerous energy, and the space between him and Sandy hummed with palpable menace. "Do not ever call me that," he snarled, each word rolling out like the crash of distant thunder. The agate-colored aura surrounding him seethed, a tempest of furious light that illuminated the sharp angles of his face and cast jagged shadows against the walls.

"Humans and their ridiculous charts, their trivial astrological signs!" His voice bit at the room, venom dripping from every syllable. He took a threatening step forward, the floor beneath him creaking in protest as if recognizing the burden of power he carried. "Do not presume to understand me, human," he spat, the corners of his lips curling in contempt. "Know your place, or you'll find yourself in great danger in my presence."

Sandy remained motionless, his eyes unwavering as they met Geminus's glare. The boy's posture, though slender and unremarkable, seemed anchored by an inner force that defied the encroaching wrath of gods. I felt a knot of admiration twist in my chest. Soren and Geminus looked at Sandy like they wanted to peel him apart, tear him open until every secret was laid bare. Yet, despite the deadly intent gathering in the room, Leopold's presence was a barrier they dared not cross.

Leopold, his typically stoic face now alight with something akin to surprise, turned his gaze to Sandy. His expression shifted, softening from steely resolve to a look touched with wonder. "You would be wise not to provoke Soren and Geminus," Leopold warned, his voice lower, tempered with an urgency that settled like smoke around us. "Those two have ended thousands of human lives purely for their amusement." I considered echoing his advice, but even as the words formed in my throat, I knew they were pointless. Sandy was beyond caution; he was walking a line that no mortal should dare.

"I know," Sandy answered, the defiance in his voice muted now, but not lost. There was something hauntingly resigned about it, a quiet recognition of his own fate. "But as you all know, my life is ending soon anyway, so what do I have to fear?" The statement hung heavily in the charged air, sinking into the silence like a stone dropped into deep water. He let the moment breathe before adding, "It is Virgilian you'll have to deal with."

A chill swept over me, realization tightening its grip on me. A tumor—I could almost see it now, its dark fingers curling through the boy's brain, leeching life and light with each passing hour. The scent of impending death hung around him, subtle but unmistakable, a whisper from the abyss. Soren had sensed it the moment we walked in, yet somehow, it was only now unfurling before me. The boy should have been frail, a whisper of what he once was, but here he stood: defiant, unyielding, more than just a pawn. Sandy was something vital, a keystone in whatever intricate puzzle Virgilian had laid.

"And I imagine," Sandy continued, his voice cutting through the charged silence like a blade, "that if you harm me, Virgilian will likely exclude you from his plan altogether." The weight of his words pressed on the room, settling like a shroud. He paused, eyes glistening with a challenge that dared them to act. "So no, I have no fear of you all at this moment. Let's see how the day plays out, shall we?" The smirk that curled at the corners of his mouth was maddeningly confident, a flame dancing before a gale.

A sharp bark of laughter threatened to spill from me—I bit it back, surprised at my own amusement. This boy, with all his audacity, had a gall that bordered on reckless genius.

"So, you do know what Virgilian's plan is, don't you?" Soren's voice slithered into the space between them, suspicion coating each word like poison. His eyes, dark and deep as the void, locked onto Sandy with a relentless stare. The boy's defiance was admirable, but here, in this room dense with godly wrath, it made him a target.

Sandy's posture remained unyielding. "I've been given very limited details on Virgilian's plan," he said, each word wrapped in a practiced nonchalance. It was a lie, one that cracked like a whip in the tense room, obvious to anyone watching. "What I do know is that I've been asked not to discuss it with you, and I have no intention of doing so."

Soren's eyes narrowed, the skin around them taut with anger. His voice dropped to a near whisper, each syllable cold enough to frost the air. "He's lying," he declared, stepping forward with the lethal grace of a predator. The room seemed to shrink as his presence swelled, a suffocating shadow draped over us. "He knows more than he's letting on."

Geminus's lips parted in a slow, wicked grin, the glimmer in his eyes betraying a deep, simmering malice. "We should squeeze his weak little body until he tells us the truth," he said, his voice a low growl, vibrating with the promise of violence. His body shifted, stretching taller and more imposing until he was an obsidian tower, each movement a deliberate proclamation of dominance. Dark, silken hair fell around his face like a lion's mane, his eyes flashing with cruel intent. Power radiated from him, sharp and stinging, the room thick with it. Sandy, in comparison, looked like a flickering candle in the face of a storm.

"Thank you," Sandy said, his tone so flippant it made Geminus pause. He cocked an eyebrow as if genuinely amused by the transformation. "I do appreciate a bit of eye candy." His eyes flitted to Soren, who had not yet shed his grotesque form. The boy's gaze flickered with mock impatience. "Perhaps you could convince your friend to put on something more appropriate? I won't be intimidated by either of you, so why don't we all just relax and wait for our host?"

The smile that curved across Soren's monstrous lips was jagged, split with sharp teeth that seemed made for tearing. He said nothing, but his eyes gleamed with something predatory. I knew the look—he was calculating, savoring the thought of future vengeance. Soren was praying that Virgilian's plan would grant him the opportunity to show Sandy what terror truly meant.

"Old ally," Soren finally spoke, a dark, knowing grin spreading as he shifted, shedding his monstrous skin for the radiant, terrifying splendor of his true form. Energy crackled like living fire around him, and the air shuddered in response. The room seemed to pulse, alive and on edge. "This place reeks of creatures who judge us for crimes they've committed themselves. Hypocrites, the lot of them. Care for a breeze?"

"Always," Geminus replied, his voice rich with amusement as he, too, let his human guise dissolve. His power unraveled around him in silken, agate-colored waves that mingled with the deeper, blood-red hues radiating from Soren. They stood together, no longer tethered by mortal disguises, their combined aura making the room tremble as if even the walls understood their place.

I watched them slip out through the window's cracked seal, a collective exhale escaping those left behind. The tension lifted, leaving the room hollow, and I felt the urge to sit beside Sandy. But the boy, eyes weary and shadowed, leaned back, his lids fluttering as he gave in to exhaustion. With a reluctant sigh, I made my way to the lower half of the house, finding Sarah Francis and Paisly clustered in a tight circle. I toyed with the idea of slipping away to find a secluded spot where I could untangle my thoughts. The centuries had not been kind when it came to my place among our kind; Soren had seen to that. His relentless cruelty had left a stain, an indelible mark that seemed to follow me like a shadow. Whenever we were near others, their gazes would turn sharp, accusatory, as if his sins were mine to bear. I understood that Soren had committed unspeakable acts, horrors that left scars on more than just flesh, but I could never grasp why they held me accountable. I had no control over him, no influence over his choices. And yet, the weight of his actions settled on me like a cloak I hadn't asked to wear.

Instead, I summoned my courage and stepped into the circle, determined to face my fears head-on. The air shifted subtly as I joined them, a ripple of awareness passing through the group. Paisly, who had been passionately describing the bioluminescent splendor and bustling community of her kind deep at the ocean's floor, fell silent for a moment, her eyes flicking to mine before she continued with less fervor. But soon, the conversation shifted unexpectedly when Sarah Francis launched into an unprompted account of Viviana and Leland.

Like Soren and me, like Lilith and Thomas, like Geminus and Ginevra, Viviana and Leland were a couple that had been together since the dawn of their existence. Sarah Francis's voice softened, tinged with both admiration and pity, as she recounted how Leland had become consumed by his work. He was nurturing the evolution of a species on a new, untamed world deep within the region known as The Thickness—a place where stardust and primordial gases churned in chaotic beauty. He had become so engrossed in his creation that he hadn't noticed when Viviana returned home cycles ago. Now, it seemed, Viviana had found solace in Pascal, Paisly's masculine counterpart. They spent their days together in effortless harmony, the sort that resembled the unity of bonded souls, even if it wasn't sanctified by the Source.

Confusion and disbelief simmered inside me as I listened. How could the Source bless them? I asked, the question slipping out before I could stop myself. My voice held a note of naive defiance. She is already part of a two.

Sarah Francis turned to me, her eyes wise and unfathomably deep, holding truths I hadn't dared to consider. "She is whatever she wishes to be," she replied, her tone gentle but firm, as if speaking to a child who had only just glimpsed the complexity of the world. "The Source need not bless every union."

I stared at her, stunned by this revelation. The words struck like lightning, electrifying my mind and shaking the foundations of everything I believed. For a moment, the room seemed to tilt, the familiar outlines of reality shifting in ways I hadn't anticipated. The Source's blessing was sanctified, the ultimate bond, creation itself. To think that it could be disregarded, that it could be broken—it was abomination to everything I knew.

Without a word, I turned on my heel, the room blurring as I moved. I pushed past the door and out into the cool expanse of night, my form dissolving into weightlessness as I drifted up to the roof. The air was crisp and thin, wrapped in the scent of cosmic dust and the whisper of ancient breezes that had circled the universe countless times.

I sat there, suspended in the quiet of the stars, my thoughts churning. Hours passed unnoticed as I grappled with this new understanding, the echo of Sarah Francis's words reverberating in my mind. No, I thought stubbornly, the denial welling up like a tidal force within me. No, it was not okay to break away from something ordained by the Source. The very idea gnawed at my core, shaking me to my essence.

I was still on the rooftop, lost in the labyrinth of my thoughts, when I saw Geminus returning from whatever reckless adventure he and Soren had embarked upon. He appeared alone, of course. No doubt, things had escalated beyond even Geminus's appetite for chaos, leaving Soren to indulge in his atrocities unchecked. Geminus moved with the effortless grace of someone who knew the world bent to his will. The night wrapped around him, the starlight catching in the strands of his dark hair, making it shimmer like a blade drawn in moonlight.

I watched as he slipped into the house below, weaving through the dim corridors until he emerged like a shadow behind Leopold, who stood just inside Seraphina's doorway. The soft glow from the room spilled out, illuminating Leopold.

I listened to every word exchanged, though I didn't need to hear them to know the truth. Seraphina allowed Geminus to give her pleasure that night, but it was Leopold she longed for. The knowledge settled uneasily within me, a strange mix of curiosity and pity twisting in me. I had never envied those who walked alone, those like Seraphina or the enigmatic yahudiyah who roamed the edges of existence, eternally solitary. I thought beings like Virgilian and Aryalis were fortunate to have found their counterparts so soon after inception. And for those of us created alongside our destined partners, it felt as though we were marked as favorites of the Source. We were gifted with eternal companionship, a bond spun from the first breath of existence itself.

There were some, like Sarah Francis, who had never known a mate, who walked alone with a serenity that seemed almost foreign to me. But I had always had Soren. Yes, he had become a problem, more volatile and unpredictable as of late, but he was mine. He had always been by my side, his presence constant, as reliable as the cycles of the stars. He would never grow so absorbed in a project or a scheme that he wouldn't notice if I were missing. The thought that he could choose to walk away, that he might decide one day not to be there, carved out a hollow in me that filled with a dread I couldn't name. It was a fear both sharp and ancient, reaching into the very essence of what I was.

□

Chapter Six

I was still perched on the rooftop, eyes fixed on the horizon where the first rays of the sun painted the sky with strokes of deep gold and rose, when I noticed Virgilian's return. His Saffire glow shimmered faintly as he approached, exuding the otherworldly energy that always surrounded him like an invisible cloak. I kept silent, letting the cool morning breeze wrap around me as he passed below, unaware of my presence. It wasn't until he entered the house and his voice resonated within its walls that I stirred, following the sound inside.

By the time I descended into the living room, the others had already gathered. Their expressions varied: curiosity from Leopold, skepticism from Paisley, an indifferent smirk from Ginevra. Virgilian's eyes flicked over each of them as he began speaking, his tone calm and authoritative. He recounted how he found Sandy and revealed his ambitious plan—to make the boy the most Source-aware human ever conceived. The pieces of the puzzle finally clicked into place. The boy's lack of fear when facing Soren, the steady defiance that shone in his eyes—it all made sense now. He had glimpsed the nightmares Soren created through Virgilian's eyes, prepared in ways we couldn't fathom.

I leaned against the wall, absorbing this revelation while Virgilian's voice threaded through the room, steady and compelling. He explained what Sarah Francis had shared with him: that the human soul, that mysterious, ineffable core we all found so intoxicating to ride, was indeed a fragment of the Source itself. It splintered off at birth and returned upon death, a tiny shard of divine essence on a cosmic journey. The explanation fit, even if it didn't feel quite right; it was the closest we'd come to solving that riddle.

As the implications sank in, I reflected on my own experiences—how many times I had succumbed to the irresistible pull of riding a human soul to the brink, reveling in that stolen ecstasy. It was a rush unlike any other, a tether to something greater, but the thought of it now filled me with a sudden, unexpected guilt.

It was Seraphina who broke my reverie, her voice cutting through the room with a sharp edge. "This might actually make a difference," she conceded, her gaze still skeptical. "But are we sure this boy is the right vessel? What if we're wasting time? I could name a dozen more suitable candidates, including one I designed myself." She leaned forward, eyes glinting with pride. "Leopold may have passed on the opportunity, but that human grew into something magnificent."
Leopold, standing just behind Virgilian, let out a dry chuckle. "Are we back to that again?"

Virgilian's expression remained unmoved as he replied, "We're using Sandy. The process has already begun, and it was his idea. Excluding him now would be in poor taste."

Ginevra, who had been listening in silence, finally spoke up. Her voice was clipped, tinged with incredulity. "So, I'm just supposed to shed a body I've nurtured for over sixty years? Some of us enjoy these human lives, you know. I've only just begun to make my mark in this one." She crossed her arms, her eyes challenging anyone to contradict her.

Leopold shook his head, a wry grin tugging at his lips. "I don't know how you do it. I can barely stand to stay in a human form past forty. The second things stop working and the aches start, I'm out."

Ginevra's lips curved into a knowing smile. "It's easier to accomplish certain things when the body is older, especially in politics. Women are taken more seriously once they're past their childbearing years. That's when their bodies become truly useful."

Leopold laughed, the sound dry and sardonic. "Well, that's the exact opposite for me. The first thirty years are prime for sports, for the thrill of competition." He flexed his fingers as if preparing for a game, his eyes twinkling with boyish excitement. I found their side conversation strange, considering the magnitude of what we were discussing, but before I could comment, Paisley's voice cut through the room like a blade.

"The Yahudiyah who dares to contact this boy's spirit will suffer for centuries," she warned, her tone heavy with foreboding. "You might damn yourself to endless torment, and the Source may not even notice. We're treading on dangerous ground, evolving the human brain beyond its limits."

Virgilian's eyes flickered with uncertainty. "We don't really know what those limits are."

"The hell we don't," Paisley snapped, frustration etching lines into her usually smooth brow. "Some of us have spent enough time studying them to know better. This isn't meddling in their wars or influencing their leaders. This is far more dangerous."

I could feel her negativity pulling the room into a spiral of doubt, the way it so often did. It forced me to counterbalance it, to be more optimistic, if only to break free from her suffocating skepticism. "But don't you see?" I interjected, my voice urgent, eyes bright with conviction. "This plan is perfect. If Sarah Francis holds the boy's soul, we can cling to her without making direct contact. We can ride him all the way back to the Source. If it fails, we hit the wall, but we won't suffer. It's as safe as it could be."

Virgilian's eyes softened with concern as he turned to me. "We can't guarantee that, though. Even if Sarah Francis rides the soul home, she could suffer. The risk is great, but it's mine to take. The boy is my friend. I will hold his soul. You can all cling to me, and if we fail, I will bear the brunt of it."

That worked for me. As long as I didn't have to touch the boy's soul directly, I was content. I almost believed the plan would succeed; the boy had impressed me.

"I wouldn't have you take such a risk for us," Paisley said softly, a rare moment of vulnerability flashing in her eyes.
"No," Leopold said, stepping forward. "We'll share the burden."

"There will be no shared burden," Paisley snapped, her voice cutting through the air like a whip. "This shouldn't even be up for debate. If the Source wanted humans to have this knowledge, it would have revealed it to them already!" Her frustration painted her cheeks a deep, stormy red. I chose to stay silent, the argument exhausting me. If the Source had a better plan, now would be the time to intervene. Almost on cue, Soren's voice broke through the tension.

"May I make a suggestion?" he said lightly, an uncharacteristic glint in his gaze.

"No," Virgilian said immediately, his tone brooking no dissent. "Your input is not required."

"You wound me, Virgilian," Soren replied with mock injury, a playful smile tugging at the corners of his mouth. "I was willing to go along with your plan, to share my essence with the human and everything." The statement sent a shiver through me. Soren, willing to share? To enlighten rather than destroy? It was unprecedented.

"You will not be sharing yourself," Virgilian said, his voice hard as stone. His eyes fixed on Soren, holding him in place. "You have done nothing since your inception that speaks of brilliance or restraint. You are the noise in the dark, the terror under their beds. You and Geminus are neither needed nor wanted in this experiment." His words landed like a hammer. "Sit in the corner and wait to see if we find a way home for you both."

A silence settled over the room, cold and sharp. Soren's expression darkened, eyes narrowing into slits of pure hatred. "Go ahead then," he hissed. "I'll look forward to seeing you suffer on the outer wall, mourning your failure. I'll enjoy every moment of it."

Before the tension could thicken further, Geminus's calm voice sliced through the air. "Your idea is brilliant, Virgilian, but it has flaws." His tone was analytical, almost detached.

"I didn't ask for your opinion," Virgilian snapped, cutting him off. I had nearly forgotten Geminus was even in the room; he had been so silent since his private encounter with Seraphina. I wondered if Ginevra knew.

Unfazed, Geminus continued, "The plan will only succeed if we all contribute—every last one of us, including Soren and me. For the boy to carry this message to the Creator, he needs knowledge from all thirteen of us. But there's one who will never participate. Aryalis will not leave her place on the wall, and without her, the boy's mind will shatter under the weight of all we impart. Humans are too fragile for this."

"I believe it will work," Sandy's voice suddenly interjected, slicing through the tense silence like a blade. His entrance startled everyone; we all turned in unison those of us in our own forms immediately shaping into human form, to the doorway where he stood, a gaunt figure backlit by the dim hallway. His skin looked almost translucent, a sickly pallor emphasizing the deep circles under his eyes. He seemed smaller, as though the weight of the knowledge shared had physically diminished him overnight. Still, there was an unmistakable fire in his gaze, a stubborn resolve that kept him upright when any ordinary human would have collapsed.

I felt a rush of admiration, tinged with an unexpected pang of dread. I believed in Virgilian's plan, but I didn't get the chance to voice my agreement before Paisley spoke, her voice as sharp and cold as a blade of ice.

"What you believe is irrelevant, boy," she said, each word clipped and unforgiving. Her eyes, usually pools of calm blue, had narrowed into hard slits. "The suffering from failure would be unparalleled."

Sandy's lips pressed into a thin line, but he didn't flinch. "And the reward for success is beyond measure," he whispered, his voice trembling slightly but still clear. The room shifted as we digested his words, a shared unease rippling through those gathered. I couldn't help but wonder if Sandy truly understood what that success meant. Did he grasp that success would almost certainly mean his own death? For us, the reward would be an unprecedented return to the Source, an end to our eons-long exile. But for him? What awaited him beyond that final barrier? I marveled at his courage, puzzled by it, yet somehow reassured.

The sudden chime of the doorbell shattered the moment, and we all tensed as the front door creaked open. Casper and Aquilus stepped into the room, their imposing forms casting long shadows across the floor. Though they were born as twins in their human guises, they were as different as night and day. Casper stood impeccably dressed, his tailored suit free of even the slightest wrinkle, eyes keen and observant under perfectly combed hair. Aquilus, on the other hand, exuded a rugged charisma with his untrimmed beard and shoulder-length hair that caught in the faint draft, moving like dark silk.

A tremor of anticipation coursed through me. Normally, Aquilus's presence would act as a lightning rod for Soren's temper. The moment the two shared a space, their volatile history crackled in the air like an impending storm, often forcing me to drag Soren away before chaos erupted. But now, there was only a strange, stifling calm. I glanced at Soren out of the corner of my eye and saw him watching Aquilus with an unreadable expression, the usual animosity absent. It felt unnatural, as though the room itself was holding its breath.

Leopold shifted uneasily, a subtle reminder of his own deep-seated rivalry with Soren, yet even he kept his silence. It was as if an invisible force had dampened the usual sparks that flew between them all, drawing a shroud of anticipation over the room.

Something was changing, I realized—a subtle shift in the balance of power or perhaps a collective realization of the stakes involved. Whatever it was, it felt significant, a turning point that none of us were prepared for. And in that tense silence, Sandy stood like a frail prophet.

"Sandy, please excuse yourself from this conversation," Virgilian said, his tone firm yet not devoid of kindness. The boy's eyes flickered with confusion, mirroring my own surprise. Why was he being dismissed now, at such a critical juncture? Before I could voice my question, Paisley interjected, her voice sharp as a blade.

"Why?" she demanded, crossing her arms over her chest and fixing Virgilian with a glare. "If he knows everything, why should he be excused?"

"Sandy, take your leave," Virgilian repeated, the finality in his tone silencing any further protest. The weight of authority in his voice left no room for argument. "We will begin with you shortly, but I need time with them first."

Sandy's shoulders drooped, and the confident light in his eyes dimmed. A shadow of hurt passed over his features, as if he'd been struck. For a moment, I thought he might resist, but then he lowered his gaze, nodded once, and left the room.

Virgilian's gaze followed Sandy's retreat until he was out of sight. When he spoke again, his voice dropped, weighted with a solemnity that sent a chill up my spine.

"He doesn't know about the soul yet," he revealed, glancing at each of us to measure our reactions.

Casper, who had been standing at the edge of the room with an expression of detached interest, straightened. "What doesn't he know about the soul?" he asked, a rare hint of curiosity breaking through his usual stoic demeanor. His brows knitted together as he sought clarity.

Virgilian took a measured breath, his eyes darkening with the gravity of the moment. He began to brief the new arrivals, repeating the details we had gone over countless times, each word charged with significance. "I haven't told him about the soul yet," he admitted. "It's the final piece. I want him to have a firm grasp of every other aspect before introducing this one. The soul's reaction to being called by name is unpredictable. I need every element in place before we take that step."

I stiffened at his words. This was the opening Soren had been waiting for—a chink in the armor of the plan that he could exploit. The moment there was doubt, Soren would pounce, disrupt, and tear the whole thing apart. I could almost feel the crackle of his anticipation, an itch beneath my skin that signaled his readiness to sow chaos. My pulse quickened with the realization that we were on the verge of losing control. Sandy was extraordinary, but even his resilience had limits. And if Soren chose to act, the entire plan would unravel before it could even begin.

I decided I couldn't stay silent any longer. The room was teetering on a knife's edge, the atmosphere dense with tension and unsaid fears. "I don't see how you can get every other piece in place," I said, my voice laced with skepticism. I felt the eyes of everyone turn toward me, the weight of their attention pressing down on me like a physical force. "Lilith and Tomas aren't here. Aryalis won't budge from the wall. The rest of us are split down the middle on this plan. For this to work, we need unity—all of us, including Soren and Geminus." I glanced at Soren, who remained silent but was now smirking in that infuriating way of his. "Whether you like it or not, Virgilian, you'll have to trust them with your experiment. And honestly, I'm not sure you can. I wouldn't blame you if you couldn't. There are too many unresolved variables."

A strained silence followed, broken only by the subtle rustle of fabric as Seraphina stood abruptly. Her sudden movement drew every eye to her, a ripple of surprise washing through the room. "I'm going to download my thoughts into this boy's head and then head home," she declared, her voice steady but laced with impatience. "If it works, wonderful. If not, so be it. Let me know what happens when you finally tell him about the soul." She shot Soren a withering look that could have stripped paint from the walls. "Virgilian has a plan, and it's a good one—or at least not the worst one I've heard. I'll contribute. I'm going first."

I watched Seraphina leave, feeling a surge of relief wash over me. She had made her decision without consulting the group, asserting her choice to go next, and if the opportunity arose, I was ready to follow in her footsteps. I silently urged her to move quickly, before the others had time to second-guess or worse, propose a vote that could disrupt our fragile consensus. The plan was already in motion; the boy had survived absorbing Virgilian. If he endured Seraphina's essence as well, it would pave the way for a third.

Positioning myself on the fringes of the room, I tuned in to the murmured conversations and guarded glances that shifted like whispers of a storm. I could sense the tension, brittle and sharp, hanging in the air. As usual, no one dared initiate a conversation that might draw in Soren. He loomed in the far corner, a figure steeped in restless energy, eyes glinting with dark intent. I could feel the turbulence in his mind from across the room, as though his thoughts were tangible things that tugged at the edges of my own. When his voice slipped into my consciousness, low and probing, I was not surprised.

Have you ever noticed that Sarah Francis is the only one of us without a masculine counterpart? His thought landed with a subtle weight, sharp enough to demand attention.

I hadn't, not until you brought it up, I replied, trying to mask the flicker of recognition that crossed my mind. It was strange, now that he mentioned it. I had considered it before, in a roundabout way—how Sarah Francis had always walked her path alone, never tethered to another soul. But I didn't want to follow this thread with Soren, not now, not when we were so close to testing Seraphina's outcome. But what difference does it make? I added, hoping to steer him away from where I knew his mind was heading.

Soren's presence simmered beside me, a silent tempest that threatened to burst. Are you starting to notice things that should have been obvious? he asked, a note of quiet insistence woven into his words.

Maybe, I admitted, the uncertainty gnawing at me, but for now, behave yourself. My response was edged with both caution and an attempt at lightness. Let's see what comes of Seraphina's time with the boy. For once, let me observe without your meddling.

I glanced at him, meeting his dark eyes with a firm yet strangely affectionate look. His expression softened, if only slightly, but I could still see the tension coiled in his posture. Just this once, Soren, I added, my voice in his mind carrying a plea I rarely let show. Let's see what happens without your... creative interference.

Hours drifted by, the room shifting through phases of silence and muted conversation. Outside, the sun journeyed across the sky, casting long shadows that crept along the floor and up the walls like silent witnesses. The air felt heavy, dense with waiting. When Virgilian finally returned, the room came alive with a collective breath held too long. His face, told us everything before he spoke a word.

"Seraphina and Sandy are resting," he announced, his voice tinged with a weariness that made the room feel colder. "The ordeal took a heavy toll on both of them."

A murmur swept through those gathered, a blend of concern and anticipation. Ginevra stepped forward, her presence commanding as always, even in this moment of uncertainty. “I’ll go next, when the boy is strong enough,” she said, the determination in her voice unwavering. “I, too, wish to return to my life.”

Disappointment twisted in my chest, an instinctive response that I quickly masked. It was selfish, I knew—coveting the next chance for myself—but I could not help it. This gamble was our best shot, maybe our only shot, and the waiting felt endless, a limbo that tested even the most patient among us.

Soren shifted beside me, his silence unsettling. He was watching Virgilian, eyes calculating, as if searching for the smallest crack in his composure. I exhaled slowly, a silent plea that this fragile truce would hold, at least long enough for us to see where Seraphina’s contribution would lead.

Virgilian nodded, "Yes, Ginevra, you should be next, followed by everyone else in human form," he said. His eyes swept slowly around the room, meeting each of ours in turn, assessing our readiness, our doubts. "Until we know if the plan is viable, there's no point in everyone waiting around here. We need to delay Soren and Geminus's turn as long as possible, at least until Lilith and Tomas arrive and make their decision. Without their participation, subjecting Sandy to Soren's memories would be needless cruelty."

His words settled over the room like a dense fog, smothering any hope of immediate action. A sense of foreboding crept up on me, cold and insistent. Days—perhaps even weeks—would pass before I'd have my turn with the boy. A hollow dread gnawed at me; the notion of keeping Soren in check for that long felt impossible. Doubts began to bubble beneath the surface of my resolve, eroding my faith in the plan.

The silence stretched thin, broken only by the sound of someone shifting their weight. "If everyone else has made their attempt, I will try again with Aryalis," Virgilian said, the weariness in his voice belied by the determination etched across his features.

"Perhaps if I spoke to her," Sarah Francis suggested, a note of calm certainty in her voice. "Saying no to you has become routine for her, Virgilian. But has anyone else tried to bring her down from the wall?"

The question hung unanswered, a silent admission of Aryalis's isolation. I have, I wanted to say. I've been to the wall many times, playing melodies with instruments shaped by the echoes of her own sounds. But I held my tongue. Soren didn't know, and I had no desire to reveal that I had a sanctuary—a place where even he couldn't reach me. Aryalis had become my refuge, the one being who didn't ask anything of me, who didn't care whether I stayed or went. Each visit had been my choice, a respite from Soren's constant, tempestuous presence. He never looked for me there; perhaps it was beneath his pride or beyond his interest.

When no one else spoke, Sarah Francis pressed on. "It's hardly surprising she has no interest," she said, her eyes narrowing with an uncharacteristic edge. "You've been her only contact for ages, Virgilian. Maybe if someone else gave her their account of this place, it might shift her perspective."

Nothing will change her mind, I thought, a pang of melancholy threading through me. Aryalis was as steady as the wall she clung to, dispassionate and distant. Each of my visits had ended the same way—with her serene and unmoved, her gaze fixed beyond the horizon as if watching worlds unravel that only she could see. My company had meant nothing to her; I was just a temporary noise in her silence.

"I want to see Sarah Francis pass through the wall," Soren declared, his voice cutting through the conversation like a blade. His eyes glinted with dark amusement, a warning sign that stirred unease in my chest. "This process is taking too long, and we all know what I'm like when I'm bored."

A flicker of relief passed through me at the thought of him leaving the house. If Soren was occupied at the wall, it would give me the freedom to observe the boy more closely, without Soren's erratic shadow looming over me.

Leopold stepped forward, his face a mask of controlled emotion. "I've been to the wall before," he admitted, glancing at Sarah Francis. "But I'll confess I never tried to bring Aryalis down. Every time I saw her, I was passing by, on my way somewhere else. She never seemed grateful for the company, so I never stayed long. But I'll take you, Sarah Francis. We can speak to her together, and I, too, would like to witness your interaction with the wall."

There was no further debate. Without another word, without even a glance from Soren in my direction—true to his nature of sharing only when it suited him—they departed. The room felt different the moment they were gone, lighter but not without tension. I exhaled, my chest loosening as if a band had been cut.

Not wasting another moment, I made my way up to the boy's den. The hallway was quiet, each step muffled by the thick, aged carpet beneath my feet. When I reached the door, I pushed it open just enough to peek inside. Sandy lay there, his body pale but breathing evenly. To my surprise, Seraphina was curled beside him, their limbs tangled in a tender, unconscious embrace. The boy's arm rested around her waist, his fingers loosely gripping the fabric of her dress, as if anchoring himself even in sleep. Her head was nestled into the crook of his neck, the soft rise and fall of their chests moving in harmony.

A swell of emotion caught in my throat—something raw and undefinable. They looked fragile, connected in a way that made the room feel sacred. I withdrew silently, closing the door with a feather-light touch.

I made my way to the roof, my favorite refuge in this house. The sky stretched endlessly above, a vast canvas of deepening blues. The quiet solitude wrapped around me like a familiar cloak, soothing the frayed edges of my mind. With a deep breath, I let my energy flow into my hands, shaping it into the elegant form of a violin. The strings shimmered with a faint glow, and I raised the bow to play, the notes resonating in my mind alone. Each sound was crystalline, alive—a private symphony that existed solely for me.

I loved these moments, hours spent drawing music from the air, each vibration rippling through my essence. To anyone who might glance up, it would seem as though I were merely miming an instrument, moving in a silent dance with the wind. But to me, every note was tangible, each chord resonating through my being as if the universe itself were humming along.

I was lost in this self-made paradise when a sudden shift in the air caught my attention. Paisley materialized beside me, her presence as quiet as the fading light. She stood there, framed by sky, her expression unreadable.

“I wish I could hear you,” she said softly, breaking the silence. There was a wistfulness in her voice, a longing that surprised me. “It’s been years since you played for us.”

The bow hovered over the strings as I paused, considering her words. The old pain of isolation surfaced, raw and unexpected. “I know how you all feel about Soren,” I replied, my tone guarded. “So, to please you, I’ve kept my distance.”

“Why not just distance yourself from him?” she asked, her voice gentle but laced with something sharper. The question pierced through me, leaving me momentarily stunned.

I turned to look at her, my eyes searching hers for answers that I knew she wouldn’t—or couldn’t—give. The suggestion felt both absurd and painful. Why would I do that? The thought of separating myself from Soren was like considering the loss of a limb, a part of me that, however flawed, was still mine.

Her expression softened, and she turned her gaze toward the horizon, where the sun bled into the sea of clouds in swathes of crimson and gold. “Play me the song you were just playing,” she said, the faintest smile ghosting across her lips. “I want to hear it.”

I studied her for a moment, weighing the unexpected vulnerability in her eyes. The question that had hung between us fell away, unspoken and unnecessary. With a nod, I drew the bow across the energy-formed strings, coaxing out a melody that only we could share. The air quivered with each note, weaving together a tune that spoke of old memories and the fleeting beauty of moments that could never last.

Chapter Seven

I played for hours, letting each note linger in the air until it dissolved into silence. The luxury of being a Yahudiyah musician was that rest was not a necessity; I could sustain my private concerts endlessly. Once, in a shroud of mourning, I played alone for over a year, refusing to share the depth of my pain with my mate, Soren. He was cycling through one of his human lives then, a span where he could experience the world in all its transient beauty, unaware of my grief. This arrangement suited me; his absence afforded me the freedom to explore the world, always lingering within the shadows, close enough should he need me, yet distant enough to taste solitude.

It was during one of these periods of exploration that I found myself drawn to the cobblestone streets of Genoa, Italy. There, a small boy named Niccolò Paganini caught my attention. His fingers, even as a child, moved with an intuition that set him apart. I whispered to his father, Antonio, as he slumbered, planting the seed of recognition in his mind. The following morning, Antonio woke with a new awareness; he marveled at his son's uncanny gift and began pushing him into rigorous practice sessions. By the age of seven, young Niccolò was already captivating small audiences, each performance a precursor of the virtuosity that would soon stun the world.

Despite his promise, I was dissatisfied with the path laid before him. His early teachers, though skilled, were insufficient for the mastery I envisioned. One night, as the city slept beneath a blanket of stars, I slipped into the room where Alessandro Rolla—then Paganini's instructor—rested. I bent over his ear and whispered truths that unsettled even me. The next day, Rolla declared to Niccolò and his family that the boy's talents surpassed what he could teach. He recommended Paganini seek other masters, unknowingly aligning his fate with my silent decree.

Paganini's fame swelled like a tide, fed by rumors and impossible performances that defied belief. Audiences gasped as he executed blistering runs, double stops, and harmonics with a precision that seemed almost otherworldly. During one of these pinnacle moments, I revealed myself to him. I materialized, not as the whisper of influence I had been, but in my true, luminous form. His eyes widened, a mixture of awe and fear, as I approached and spoke: "I am the spirit that animates your strings, the unseen partner in every note. Follow my commands, and you will know a life unrivaled."

He nodded, unable to resist the allure of the promise. It was then that I allowed myself to merge with his instrument, manifesting as a violin of unparalleled beauty, carved from my essence. The sound we produced together—a timbre both haunting and divine—was like nothing ever heard before. It was why audiences swore he had bargained with the devil, mistaking me for a darker force. It stung, that accusation. I was no devil, no damned soul; that confusion was born of Soren, my mate, who reveled in his own shadowy legend.

The years swept by like the crescendo of an accelerating symphony. Paganini and I moved as one, crafting music that defied mortal limits. But when Soren shifted out of his human form, his presence returned, malevolent and unyielding. I felt him then, a dark specter within the marrow of my existence. He was jealous of the attention I gave my human protégé, a jealousy that corroded Niccolò's very being. Paganini's health began to crumble, piece by piece—each ache and affliction a deliberate act of Soren's will. His long fingers grew skeletal; his complexion turned ashen. The public marveled at his gauntness and the feverish gleam in his eyes, weaving their tales of infernal pacts. They could not know that I fought silently against Soren's poison, hoping to prolong what time we had left.

Despite my pleas for mercy, Soren demanded an end. He would not let Paganini slip quietly into death; he wanted him to suffer. And suffer he did—teeth rotting, his voice stolen by relentless laryngitis, fingers once nimble now trembling. Still, I clung to him, selfishly unwilling to let go of the music we made together. It was only when his body could no longer cradle the bow, when his hollow eyes found mine in a silent plea for release, that I surrendered. Soren, ever vigilant, claimed him that very night, extinguishing his life without ceremony.

The world was left stunned and bereft, clinging to the stories of dark deals as they mourned. The Catholic Church, swayed by whispers of infernal bargains, denied him a Christian burial, leaving his remains to linger above consecrated ground for years. Only later, with the weight of memory softened by time, was his body allowed a place to rest—a late mercy in a life dictated by shadows.

In my grief—or perhaps out of a defiant desire to punish Soren—I played my violin ceaselessly for over a year, letting the mournful strains bleed into the silence of my solitude. Each note was a protest, a lament, an accusation that resonated beyond the boundaries of time. When the final chord faded, leaving an echo that haunted the air, I found myself changed. A restless longing gnawed at me, an urge to be more than a mere player of music. I began slipping into the guise of instruments, even when no musician's hands coaxed sound from me.

I would sit, disguised as the most famous relics of melody, in the shadowed corners of museums and gilded halls. The Stradivari, the Steinways, the Guarneri del Gesù—they all became my masks. Visitors passed by, eyes full of awe, unaware that the soul within those polished veneers was mine. It was a new kind of performance, silent yet profound, my existence hidden in plain sight as I relished the shared reverence between humans and their instruments.

I was still lost in thought about Paganini, haunted by the torment he endured because I chose him. He was such an extraordinary talent that my admiration blinded me, smothering my better judgment. Of course Soren would torture him—I should have known that from the start. Selfish, the word echoed within me, a relentless whisper I tried to silence. He was only human, I reminded myself. When our time on this world ends, and I find another species worthy of my music, Paganini will be forgotten. Or so I tried to convince myself.

I was there on the rooftop when Seraphina finally took her leave. Her limousine waited only a moment before she slipped out of the house and disappeared into the night, her silhouette tense and hurried. Even from a distance, I could see the strain on her face, and I wondered why her time with the boy had affected her so deeply.

Through the window, I watched as Virgilian prepared for Ginevra to go next. I kept my distance, avoiding the others as she took her turn. For hours, they sat in the old chair—Ginevra curled up on his lap, Sandy braced beneath her. I could feel the weight of their session pressing down on him, the way each encounter seemed to drain more life from his already frail body. I wondered, not for the first time, if he would survive long enough for all of us to have our chance.

After Seraphina's session, we could hear his thoughts slipping out in disjointed fragments, stray messages projected into the minds of anyone nearby. Learning to control thought-projection, to aim your messages at one person instead of scattering them randomly, is a skill that takes years to master. But Sandy—remarkably—had it under control in minutes.

When he was finally done with Ginevra, he rose from the chair with an eerie sense of authority. He was still dying, his body wasting away before our eyes, but his mind had sharpened into something formidable.

Finally, I lowered the violin, letting its last note drift into silence, dissolving back into the nothingness from which it had come. From the rooftop, I looked down and saw Aquilus standing in the garden below, the moonlight sketching silver along the edges of his form. For a moment, I thought of ignoring him, and perhaps he would ignore me too. But of course, that wasn't to be.

"I'm sure whatever you were playing was… remarkable," he said, his gaze fixed somewhere beyond me, refusing to meet my eyes.

"You couldn't have heard that," I said. "I play only for myself."

"But even without hearing, I could feel it," Aquilus replied, his eyes reflecting a deep understanding. "I knew it was a masterpiece."

"It was a piece composed by an old student of mine," I said softly, the weight of sadness evident in my voice. I was unprepared for the vulnerability in his next question.

"How did Soren kill him?" he asked, each word steeped in compassion.

"Slowly," I replied, the memory sharpening, each note of pain ringing clear. "Very slowly."

Aquilus nodded, the gesture carrying the heaviness of unspoken sympathy. "I’m sure it was hard to endure," he said.

"I’m sure it was harder on him," I answered, my tone harsher than I intended, as if absolving myself would lessen the guilt I carried.

Aquilus looked away, his gaze drifting to the tangle of wildflowers and ivy that adorned the garden. "Sometimes we love people beyond all reason," he said, his voice distant. "We can’t let go, even when everything tells us it’s time."

It struck me that he wasn’t speaking to me anymore, but to some unseen specter from his own past. I felt like an intruder, eavesdropping on a conversation meant for the silence of the night.

My relationship had every reason, I thought defensively. We were creations of the Source itself; surely, Aquilus and everyone else should understand that. But as he stood there, his profile outlined by the moon's pale glow, caught between shadow and light, I realized that understanding might not be as simple as I had always believed.

"Perhaps I'm misunderstanding," I ventured, my voice barely above a whisper. "Do you think your bond with Casper will end as it began—here on this planet—when we're finally free to leave?"

Aquilus shifted, the movement subtle but enough to reveal the tension beneath his composed exterior. "Of course," he said, a little too quickly for my liking. He exhaled, then continued, "Our bond was forged out of necessity. Our shared interests and mutual disinterest in everything else aligned perfectly for this journey. But now that it's coming to an end, we'll find our solace elsewhere—alone or with others."

I stared at him, searching for any crack in his certainty. "I don't understand how it's so easy for you," I said, my tone edged with disbelief.

“That’s because you were created with Soren,” Aquilus replied, his voice gentle yet unwavering. “I understand—you find it difficult to imagine existing without him. It’s as if separation itself defies your nature.”

“It isn’t natural for me,” I said, my voice dropping to a murmur.

“And yet, you’ve managed it so many times,” he countered. “Every time you take the shape of an instrument and linger in that form for years, you live in solitude.”

I thought of the times Aquilus spoke of—those moments when I could transform into an exquisite instrument, flawless and captivating, lying motionless yet admired by thousands. I did nothing to earn their praise, yet their reverence washed over me like a balm. In those moments, I felt an unparalleled peace, existing in a state of serene stillness. I could spend months without a single intrusive thought, simply being—a silent masterpiece basking in quiet adoration. But that tranquility never lasted as long as I wished. Sooner or later, reality would intrude, and the weight of my true nature would draw me back from that perfect stillness.

"When I am still, the world is at peace," I said.

"No," Aquilus replied, his voice sharp. "Your world is at peace when you are still. Meanwhile, Soren roams unchecked, without conscience. Not that you offer him any moral compass when you're with him."

"Soren can't be controlled," I shot back. "He has to be lured, coaxed. I acknowledge him, even when I'm playing or pretending to be something else."

Aquilus's gaze hardened. "And that keeps the peace in your little world, no matter the cost to everyone else."

"The 'everyone else' is not my responsibility," I replied coolly. "I create vibrations, I support my mate. That is all I am required to do."

He nodded slowly, as if conceding the point, but his eyes told me he still believed I was fooling myself. The silence that followed was thick, filled with the echoes of truths we both struggled to admit.

The conversation took me back to another time, another place—long before Earth existed, on the very first world we shaped after crafting Animism, our home. In that primordial age, there were no source-aware beings besides us; we hadn't yet imagined life beyond our own essence. It was just Soren and me, standing side by side, watching Aquilus as he toiled on Tomas's creation—the entity we came to call Pokok.

Everyone experimented on Pokok. It was where Paisley first conjured oceans, where Aryalis played symphonies with storm clouds. It was where Leopold and Leticia raced around the planet for the first time, laughter trailing behind them like comet tails. Soren and I watched, captivated, as Aquilus planted the first trees and channeled his energy to make them grow. It was breathtaking. We couldn't stop; the three of us planted thousands of trees within hours, covering Pokok in a lush green tapestry. Together, we brought the first forests into being.

Now, we could barely manage a polite conversation. How things had changed.

Or had we changed? As the thought unfolded, a memory surfaced—an early problem with planting so many trees on Pokok. The trees soon overtook the small planet, leaving little space for anything else. But that didn't deter Soren. Driven by an insatiable need, he kept planting, nurturing them to grow larger and more imposing with each passing day. You see, Soren hadn't found his purpose yet. Most of us hadn't. He struggled to define what he was bringing to the universe, a universe that was still so young and untested.

His tricks and pranks, designed to unsettle or amuse, were ineffective among the Yahudiyah, who never feared or faltered. Purpose eluded him, and for a while, he clung to the idea that he could be the master of trees—more formidable than Aquilus himself. Yet, where Aquilus understood the essence of growth intuitively, as if it pulsed in his very being, Soren only mimicked what he had learned. He could only create what Aquilus had already shown him, and that limitation gnawed at him, turning wonder into frustration.

His obsession consumed him. He continued to plant, continued to expand the endless forests long after they were needed. We hadn't grasped the concepts of life and death then; nothing on Pokok died. The trees grew endlessly, ancient giants that stretched toward the skies, their roots tangling beneath the surface and stealing any room for new creations. Other projects on Pokok dwindled, then ceased altogether. The planet was surrendered to the dominion of the trees.

Fortunately, Tomas and Tabitha were endlessly prolific, weaving new worlds into existence. It was easy for others to move their work to different planets. But Pokok had taught us all an essential lesson about balance, ambition, and the unchecked spread of life. Before Earth, Soren, Aquilus, and I would still visit Pokok from time to time. We loved its towering trees and the sense of ancient life that thrived there, even after the other Yahudiyah had abandoned it. Against all odds, life had flourished. Over billions of years, a society emerged—intelligent, harmonious, living in peace and reverence for the towering giants that had once been our creation. Pokok had become a sanctuary, a place of free thinkers who knew neither war nor harm to the forests they cherished. Before Earth, it was our favorite refuge beyond the bounds of home.

But now, uncertainty gnawed at me. How would they receive us? More troubling still, how would Soren behave? Once, he had been revered as a god, celebrated for his humor and playful, harmless pranks. But those pranks were no longer harmless, and his recent release from his earthly prison cast a shadow over my thoughts. Would he channel his past mischief into something uplifting, or would his pent-up energy morph into something more destructive? A sudden pang of worry for the inhabitants of Pokok shot through me, swift and piercing. I banished the thought, replacing it with any distraction I could muster.

I brought my focus back to the present—to Aquilus, who stood with a calm that defied the storm inside me. Searching for words that would mask my unsettled mind, I finally spoke, trying for a note of lightness. "Pretending to be an instrument... I imagine that's what it must feel like to be a tree. You don't need to move much to be vital, to contribute to the world around you."

"Is that what you think you're doing? Contributing to your environment?" Aquilus's tone was sharp, almost mocking. "And Soren—he's contributing too?"

"Yes," I replied. "Soren is contributing. Now that we know the Source has been here all along, living human lives just as we have, it's clear that Soren wouldn't be free to act as he does if the Source didn't allow it. Can you say that all your actions have been honorable since we arrived?"

"Soren is not contributing!" Aquilus roared, his voice reverberating through the space. "And for you to stand there and defend him, knowing everything he's done, over and over…" He broke off, as if the words themselves were bitter. "It's an insult. To me. To everyone."

"You say that as if I've ever had a choice," I replied, my voice low, defensive.

"You've always had a choice," he shot back. "But as long as everyone sees him as the monster, you get to keep playing the innocent."

"What does that even mean?" I shouted, anger flaring."

Aquilus held my gaze, his expression hard. "How is it that you've gone this long without realizing that Soren isn't the only villain in your story?"
"I am not a villain," I shot back. "I've helped humanity understand vibrations, taught them to turn sound into art—magical art."

"And you've stood by, time after time, while Soren mutilated your own disciples," Aquilus replied, his voice cold.

"They're just humans!" I screamed. "We'll leave this place soon, and none of this will matter. If humans were truly precious to the Source, they wouldn't die so easily. We've all been here too long! This place has made monsters of us all, Aquilus—you included. You've done things here that would shatter any sense of morality."

"There was nothing I could do to stop him," I said, finally, my voice breaking.

Aquilus's eyes hardened. "Have you ever even considered trying?" His words sliced through me, cold and accusing. "You've never even tried. What he did at the campground is all over the news. Sarah Francis said he spent the night in the hospital, killing babies and riding their souls to the wall. Babies," he repeated, voice trembling with fury.

"He rides babies because it lessens the withdrawal," I replied, my tone flat, clinical.

Aquilus stared at me, unblinking, his gaze like ice pressing into my skin. He searched my face, as if he might find some hidden flicker of remorse, but I offered him none. At last, he spoke again, his voice hollow. "No… you're no monster. Even monsters have something they care about."

I bristled, a retort forming on my tongue—I have things I care about, Aquilus. But before I could say anything, a pulse rippled through my mind, sharp and insistent. We were being summoned. By the boy.

I wondered what it felt like for Soren to be called like this—summoned by a mere human child, his powers flickering like a spark compared to Soren's inferno. But I didn't have to wonder long. Soon, we stood before Sandy, watching as he dressed down Ginevra, his voice thin but unyielding as he held her accountable for her mate's chaos. When he finished, he glanced at each of us in turn, laying out the order of his next few "sessions." Unsurprisingly, Soren's name was still nowhere on the list.

At that moment, I felt a prickling sensation in my mind, Soren's voice pushing through with familiar disdain. Am I supposed to hang around like a servant, waiting for this boy to decide when I'm needed?

Of course not, I projected back, lacing my response with a hint of exasperation. Find something harmless to get into, but no more souls. The chaos you caused at the hospital and the campgrounds is more than enough for now. Go haunt something—quietly.

Why does everyone think they can tell me what to do? he shot back, irritation rippling through his words like heat. His defiance was tangible, a dark pulse simmering at the edge of my mind.

I steadied myself, recalling Aquilus's words—Even monsters have something they care about. Now was not the time to give Soren orders. He would only rebel by doing something worse.

I'm not telling you, I replied, keeping my tone calm, almost pleading. I'm asking. Just behave for a few days. This could all be over soon. We can go home, and then you'll be free to terrorize the universe again—not just this small, insignificant planet.
Without another word between them, Soren was gone, off to cause havoc she was sure. Not wanting to get into another confrontation, I slipped out of the house when I heard it would be days until my turn with the boy. So back to the patio I went, back to my violin and my own thoughts.

I felt Soren's presence sooner than I expected—sooner than I wanted. A familiar chill prickled along the edges of my awareness, and a faint pulse of irritation tightened in my essence. He had returned already. I wasn't pleased.

I did what I always did when he lingered nearby and I had no desire to speak with him: I ignored him. I kept playing, my fingers moving across the strings with deliberate focus, my gaze fixed ahead as if he were nothing more than a shadow on the periphery of my vision. The melody was soft, barely audible, a private refrain meant only for myself. Moments slipped by as I played, refusing to acknowledge him, indifferent to whether he felt slighted or dismissed.
Eventually, he drifted away—not gone, just deeper into the house. I stayed on edge, bracing myself for the confrontation I was sure he'd bring, but to my surprise, it never came. Hours passed. Geminus had come and gone, and the boy was finally resting again. And I caught the first peek of Tomas and Lilith. Good I thought, they have finally arrived.

I found Soren in the den, watching the twins, Casper and Aquilus, as they slept. He stood in the shadows, unnervingly still, his gaze fixed on them with an intensity that made my skin prickle. I didn't know what he intended, but I knew I wanted no part of it. The air around him felt charged, like a storm about to break.

Quietly, I slipped out of the house, catching a gust of wind as I took to the skies. I headed for the wall, where I knew Aryalis would be waiting, her steady presence a welcome reprieve from the dark tension I'd left behind.

Chapter Eight

I found her easily enough, as always, hovering near Virgilian's imposing presence, close to the wall, her silhouette blurred in the half-light. Aryalis's song drifted around her, weaving through the air in undulating waves, subtle at first, but strong enough to shape the clouds and stir the wind into gentle spirals. Her voice was like the whisper of a distant storm, powerful and unyielding, humming with a resonance that filled the space between us. She didn't stop singing when I arrived; she never did. It was her way of inviting me in, leaving room for me to find my place in the melody.

Taking a breath, I joined her, layering my own vibration with hers, matching her tone until our voices intertwined. With a thought, I conjured an entire symphony of phantom instruments—strings and horns and flutes that shimmered like mist in the air around us, adding depth to the rising swell of sound. High above the clouds, we became the music, our voices merging to fill the sky with harmonies too intricate and strange for human ears to fully grasp.

The world below was oblivious, unaware of the concert unfolding in the heavens. Our voices spiraled together in complex patterns, answering, countering, intertwining, each note a part of a grand, wordless conversation. For hours, we celebrated each other through sound, shaping melodies that echoed emotions we couldn't name. Joy, sorrow, longing, wonder—each thread of harmony was a memory, a promise, a secret shared in the language of song.

When we finally stopped, I spoke. "Virgilian's plan has merit," I said, breaking the silence between us.

She sighed, a sound of exasperation slipping into the wind. “Not you too. First Virgilian, then Leopold, even Sarah Francis of all people—and now you come to try to convince me to go to the surface?”

“I honestly believe this plan will work,” I said, a note of insistence in my voice. “We’re going home soon, Aryalis. There’s so much down there—so much you’ll miss if you don’t at least take one small look.”

“I’ve regretted nothing so far,” she replied, her tone calm and resolute, “and I doubt I’ll regret anything after we leave this place. I’m glad you think the plan will work. Good. I hope it does. I’ll be here, waiting, when the wall opens.”

“And then what?” I pressed. “We just go home as if nothing happened?”

She looked at me, her gaze steady. “Yes. We go back, and we continue as we always have.”

Her answer sat heavily with me, and I was quiet for a long moment, watching her. Finally, I asked, "And you're completely unconcerned with how they'll perceive our actions when we return?

She gave a small, dismissive shrug. "I am completely unconcerned," she replied, unbothered. "And you shouldn't be either. This wasn't an assignment we signed up for. We didn't choose to be trapped here. Whatever was done… it wasn't our fault. I doubt it's of any real consequence to the universe."

Her words hung in the air between us, both reassuring and unsettling. The idea that all this—our time here, the things we'd done, the lives we'd touched—could be so easily dismissed felt both comforting and strange. "When this is done," she continued, her voice soft but insistent, "and we finally get to go home, it will be as it was before. You and Soren. Virgilian and I. We'll all go back to our usual pursuits." Her gaze held a faraway gleam, as if she could already see it—our lives slipping back into place, effortless as a celestial current.

I could feel the truth of her words settling over me like a half-remembered dream. I saw us back in our own realm, immersed in the music that had once filled our days, our thoughts. Back then, that was our only calling: to attune ourselves to the pulse of the universe, to listen and respond, sometimes in solitude, sometimes together. Daily, we would surrender ourselves to the source, allowing it to shape our melodies, to fill us with something vast and unknowable, yet infinitely familiar.

Occasionally, we ventured further, visiting distant planets, savoring the strange newness that blossomed across the universe. We were explorers, yes, but never creators. We left that labor—the forging of stars, the delicate stitching of atmospheres—to others who were born for such roles. It was work too structured, too bound to purpose. Virgilian and Soren weren't even explorers; they drifted through the cosmos like leaves on the wind, curious but unburdened, conversationalists with no agenda beyond their own amusement.

We had no responsibilities like Paisley and Seraphina, no grand designs to shape civilizations or guide the fates of fledgling species. We came only when our presence was wanted, arriving in the ripe silence of worlds that were ready for music, for storytelling, for the delicate resonance of art. Our place was always after the forming, after the making, when a planet was ready to breathe and sigh and sing. And never had we lingered this long. Never had our presence left such a deep imprint.

Now, in this strange, prolonged residency, I felt the weight of our influence in ways I had never known. It was as though we were becoming something else, some other kind of beings, as if our essence was being reshaped by the gravity of this place, this purpose. And yet, I couldn't shake the yearning to return—to return to that drifting, ephemeral life, where we were only ever guests, never anchors.

Part of me wanted to give in to her assurances, to let her words wrap around me like a comforting spell. I wanted to believe that she was right—that when we finally left this place, all would settle back into familiar patterns, that these new, turbulent emotions would dissolve with time, fading as memories fade. Surely, the weight of living human lives, with all their messy, intense feelings, would lift once we returned to the endless drift of our own existence.

But thoughts of Soren wouldn't allow it. The image of him now refused to reconcile with any vision of our old life. I could feel it, an immutable truth lodged like a splinter in my mind: Soren was beyond any simple return. Whatever he had become, it went deeper than mere change. It was evolution—an evolution that felt cold and unnatural, as if he had shed the very core of who he once was.

The being I had once called my life-mate, my constant companion across the ages, was gone. In his place was something… altered, something darker. The lightness in him—the curiosity that had once led him to wander the stars without a care—had twisted into something sharper, hungrier. I'd seen it in the way he moved, as though gravity itself bent differently around him now. He was no longer the Soren I had known, but something that, given time, could become a threat, a wound in the fabric of the universe.

I tried to push this truth away, to bury it beneath layers of hope and denial. But it kept surfacing, stubborn and unyielding, like a dark note echoing through my mind. Soren's transformation wasn't something I could ignore or reason away. It was a fundamental shift, like the beginning of a storm that one could only watch as it grew closer, knowing full well it would leave devastation in its wake.

And so I was caught, suspended between my desire to believe in a return to the past and the gnawing certainty that something irreversible had taken root. I wanted to trust that we would one day escape the pull of this place, that we would drift back into the quiet rhythms of our lives. But deep down, I knew that the universe would never be quite as it was. And perhaps, neither would I.

Lost in my thoughts, I hadn't even noticed when Aryalis slipped away. It wasn't until I caught a glimpse of her scarlet light fading into the distance that I realized—to her, our conversation had already ended. No farewell, no parting words. As always, she was just... gone.

I returned to the house just in time to overhear that Geminus had already gone. His session had been brief, and he'd left in a huff, visibly frustrated. I found myself wondering what might have rattled him so quickly when, out of nowhere, Sandy's thoughts brushed against mine with a gentle, almost shy inquiry: How was your concert?

The question startled me, not only for its suddenness but for the warmth behind it. Magnificent, I replied, sending the thought back to him with the same quiet intensity. In that moment, all I could feel was joy—pure and uncomplicated. I didn't know how he had figured out where I'd been, and I didn't care. The simple fact that he possessed this gift, that he was learning to reach out to me with it, was enough to fill me with a deep sense of wonder.

When it was suggested that Leopold would go next for his endurance training, I wholeheartedly agreed. His body was failing, but his mind had a resilience that deserved to be nurtured. Perhaps this was a way to keep him grounded, to give him something to hold onto as his strength faded.

For the next few hours, Soren and I moved through the house as if we were no different from the others, blending into the daily rhythms around us. I savored the rare sense of belonging, and the unspoken truce that seemed to settle over the household. No one pressed us, no one dredged up old grievances or animosities. It was as if, for a little while, we could simply be—unburdened by the weight of our history, free to exist in the moment.

After Leopold's session with the boy, the change in Sandy was unmistakable. He might have been frail in body, but his spirit shone with a strength that was nearly tangible, a quiet resilience that made him seem ready for anything. At one point in the day, he reached out to me with a soft projection, his voice brushing my mind: Will you play for me? Just for us—something only we can hear.

I was more than happy to oblige. I took up my violin, letting the bow drift over the strings, crafting melodies just for him. I played as they discussed the plans for the coming days, my music a private thread of sound winding through the air between us. I played while he spoke of his "double snuggle" scheme, his tone light but his eyes filled with a mischief that only he and I seemed to understand.

When the idea of this "double snuggle" was first mentioned, I could practically feel Soren bristle. The very thought of it set his teeth on edge, filled him with a simmering rage he barely managed to contain. As expected, he slipped out of the house shortly after, his exit. I didn't care where he went. A calm had settled over the house, a rare and precious peace that I was in no hurry to see shattered.

With Soren gone, the atmosphere felt almost weightless, as if his departure had lifted an unseen pressure from the air. I continued to play, letting each note carry a little more warmth, a little more joy, filling the room with melodies meant only for Sandy and me. It felt like sharing a secret, a quiet rebellion against the tension that seemed to shadow us all.

Later, I retreated to the roof once more and played for myself, letting the music stretch and wander, untethered by purpose. Hours slipped by as I projected the sound to Sandy, hoping it might reach him in his sleep. I wasn't sure if he could hear me—his mind felt cluttered, tangled with thoughts and dreams I couldn't fully perceive—but just in case, I played on, letting each note carry a wish for his peace, his strength.

Meanwhile, the “double snuggle” took longer than the others, and I couldn’t help but worry they might be pushing the boy’s mind too far, overwhelming him with too much power, too quickly. But to my relief—and a spark of delight—he not only survived, he awoke with more vigor than I’d ever seen in him. His eyes shone with an energy that seemed almost uncontainable, and he demanded that the twins help him with his garage and his yard, his voice brimming with purpose.

I spent the day watching them work, shaping the yard into a small paradise. The boy’s laughter mingled with the sounds of digging and planting, filling the air with a sense of renewal. Flowers sprang up where there had been bare soil, and vines twisted along the fence, their leaves bright and green against the wood. In a matter of hours, the yard transformed, as if the boy’s very spirit had seeped into the earth, bringing it to life.

As I watched, a deep contentment settled over me. For once, I could simply enjoy the sight of him thriving, unburdened by the usual weight of worry. The music continued to hum within me, notes echoing the rhythm of the day, harmonizing with the gentle transformation below.
Soren settled beside me on the roof, silent as a shadow. Together, we watched the others working in the yard below, their figures moving through the dim evening light. After a moment, Soren's thoughts pressed into my mind, his presence sharp and tense. I don't trust the boy, he projected.

You don't trust anyone, I replied, my tone calm, almost amused, though I could feel his distrust prickling against my own.

This is different, he insisted, his gaze narrowing as he followed the boy's movements. Something is off. How is this one human—out of all of human history—able to do what he's done? How does he command Yahudiyah as if he's drawing power directly from the Source? And why is no one questioning his authority?

Because we just want to go home, I answered, a note of weariness creeping into my voice. No one cares about the 'why' or the 'how,' Soren. Only you. And you only care because you're always looking for a way to tear the plan apart. As usual.

Before he could respond, we saw it—the boy's sudden collapse. He fell as though some invisible weight had crushed him, his body crumpling to the ground. The others rushed to him immediately, gathering his limp form and carrying him inside with a frantic urgency. I felt an instinctive urge to go to him as well, to check if he was breathing, if his eyes still held that strange, resilient light. But I held myself back, knowing that any show of concern would be one betrayal too many for Soren.

It was then that I caught the first hints of Lilith in Tomas, lingering just beyond the edge of the rooftop, hovering close but staying out of sight. My first thought was relief—joy, even. They were here. They would play their part. With their help, we were all but certain to pour every known truth of the universe into this boy. From my vantage point, I watched as the others tended to him with a tenderness that bordered on reverence. Their hands moved carefully, bathing him, dressing him in fresh clothes, and laying him to rest as though he were some fragile, precious artifact of an ancient world. Later, after he'd eaten and drifted into an uneasy sleep, the Yahudiyah gathered in the adjoining room, murmuring in low, worried voices. Soren, as usual, was the first to speak, his words cutting through the tension like a blade.

"If he dies before we're finished, this has all been a colossal waste of time," he said coldly, his gaze hard and unfeeling.

Paisley frowned, her expression thoughtful. "I believe his sessions with those in human form have taken the greatest toll on him," she mused. "But we're past that now. Leopold has given him resilience and determination, though the illness still lingers. Perhaps Capriana going next will grant him peace and tranquility. To endure Soren as long as she has, she must possess a level of inner serenity the rest of us can only dream of."

Peace and tranquility? I thought, nearly laughing aloud at the absurdity of it. What made them believe that was my contribution? If they only knew the thoughts churning within me, they'd understand that there was no peace or serenity to be found here, only a restless storm.

Beside me, Soren's gaze flicked to Paisley, his eyes narrowing. Why don't you go next, Paisley? he thought privately, his suspicion pressing against my awareness like a thorn. She had been here longer than most of us, yet she kept avoiding her turn. Why wasn't she volunteering? What was she waiting for?

Soren bothers you because you lack a sense of humor, I said out loud, a smirk tugging at my lips in an attempt at levity. His antics are just that—self-amusement, nothing more.

The words felt hollow, even to me. Not long ago—days, perhaps weeks—I might have believed them. I might have laughed at Soren's barbs, rolled my eyes at his needling remarks. But now, with the boy lying fragile and feverish in the next room, Soren's relentless cynicism felt heavier, darker. And my own defenses, once so sturdy, were beginning to wear thin.
"He entertains himself with cruelty," Sarah Francis interjected from behind us, her voice as cool and sharp as a blade. "He's cruel, and you tolerate it."

"He's only cruel to the weak," I shot back, my tone hardening. "And I have no love for the weak. If I didn't believe this boy was our way off this forsaken planet, I'd kill him myself for the weakness he's showing." I kept my voice steady, hoping I sounded convincing, but Soren's raised eyebrow told me he wasn't buying it. I ignored him, pressing on as if I hadn't noticed.

"Soren isn’t cruel; he’s superior," I concluded, letting my voice turn cold and final. "There’s a distinction."

Leopold cleared his throat, breaking through the tension. "I have to be honest," he said, his voice thoughtful. "I’ve often wondered how someone like you can tolerate someone like him. I’ve seen you sit as still as a violin, letting yourself be played by the world’s most renowned musicians, never once complaining. And yet, this… beast haunts the same opera house. How do you endure it?"

With deep denial, I thought, a flicker of something sharp and uncomfortable twisting inside me. I’ve been in deep denial.

But I kept my face impassive, allowing only the faintest shrug. "We all have our pleasures," I replied dismissively. "He enjoys frightening humans out of their wits. I don't mind his hobbies; they rarely interfere with my plans, and when they do, I adjust. It's straightforward, really. We're not here for a long time; we're here for a good time, aren't we?" I used Leopold's old favorite phrase, hoping he'd recognize it as an olive branch, a subtle attempt to lighten the mood.

"You're here for a good time, apparently," Virgilian cut in, his voice cold and biting. "The rest of us see Soren for what he is—a monster. You'd do well to consider him from another perspective."

I am, Virgilian, I thought, feeling the weight of his words sink in. I'm beginning to see what you all see. But what am I supposed to do about it?

I met his gaze and replied, sharper than intended. "What's he going to do? Kill my favorite human? Been there, done that. At least I've learned not to form attachments to things that die so easily. I should thank him for that lesson. I'm over it. Maybe you should try getting over it too, Virgilian. Find something else to bicker about."

I turned to Soren, a faint, calculated smile on my lips. "We're heading out. I'll be back in time for my session with the boy." Without waiting for a response, I led Soren out, knowing this conversation was going nowhere productive. More importantly, I knew Sandy was listening, though no one else seemed to notice. He needed rest, and this bickering wasn't helping.

Soren allowed me to lead, something he rarely did. Once we were outside, I caught a pocket of wind and guided us high into the sky, letting the night air clear the remnants of the tense conversation. We drifted for hours, Soren strangely content to follow, his silence like an unspoken truce. I kept us close to the house, circling just beyond sight, unwilling to stray too far from Sandy. I wanted to be near in case he signaled he was ready for our session—or worse, if he found himself in some kind of trouble.

The slow, looping flight reminded me of the days when Soren and I would take turns slipping in and out of human form, trading our ethereal nature for flesh and bone. Back then, I could drift great distances before Soren would call me back, needing some feat he could only perform with the help of a Yahudiyah. I'd learned to keep a sense of him, a subtle awareness of his proximity, tethering my own freedom to the invisible pull of his presence. Now, I used that same skill to keep Sandy's mind within comfortable reach, careful not to let Soren see where my attention was really directed.

Or so I thought, until his voice brushed against my mind. I see what you're doing, he projected, his tone laced with a quiet suspicion.

I kept my expression neutral, my mind as still as possible, but he pushed on.

This boy—this human—is changing everyone, he continued, his thoughts pressing uncomfortably close. I can feel it.

I tried not to react, not to let him sense the way his words cut into me. How could I explain to him—the mate I'd shared a billion years with—that it wasn't just the boy changing. I was changing. Some veil had lifted from my eyes, and now, all I could see was the monster everyone else had been trying to show me. I couldn't say it. I didn't have the words to tell him he was no longer who I thought he was.

I said nothing, allowing us to continue floating on the wind, my silence a flimsy shield between us. After a long moment, Soren took command, shifting the currents beneath us and guiding us back toward the house, his grip on our direction tightening as if he could sense my retreat. I felt a flicker of worry for Sandy's safety, but I reminded myself that Leopold and the others would protect him. Even if Soren turned on him, they'd stand in his way.

And then, in a sudden, startling realization, I knew with certainty that I'd stand in his way too. For the first time in my existence, I understood that I would protect a human from Soren if it came to that.

When we stepped inside, we were hit by a wave of unexpected projections—images, emotions, memories spilling from Sandy's mind. The boy was broadcasting his life story to everyone in the room, his memories flashing like scenes from a half-forgotten dream. We arrived just in time to witness his birth, a blur of light and warmth, followed by fleeting images of him growing up—small and delicate compared to his brothers, who towered over him with a careless strength. He was always the smallest, the most fragile, a subtle target in a family that valued physical power.

If Yahudiyah could weep, I would have done so when I saw his father's face—cold, dismissive, a wall of indifference that had defined Sandy's childhood. Sandy's frailty had forged an invisible barrier between them, an unspoken rejection that had seeped into every part of the boy's being. I felt the echo of his loneliness, his sense of never quite belonging, and something in me ached.

As Sandy's memories continued to unfold, I sensed Soren's growing discomfort beside me. His usual cold detachment flickered, his mind tightening as if trying to shield himself from the boy's pain. But I allowed myself to take it all in, each memory a quiet, poignant reminder of why this boy mattered. And for the first time, I felt a simmering defiance toward Soren.

Sandy had spent most of his life wrapped in isolation. He traveled alone, attended appointments alone, even navigated the daunting process of registering for college by himself. Every milestone he reached was shadowed by solitude, each small victory weighed down by the aching absence of someone to share it with. But Sandy's pain ran deeper than loneliness—it was laced with betrayal. Robert Earl, the old man entrusted with his care, had deceived Sandy's parents about his intentions. And though they knew Robert Earl was lying, they handed over custody of their son anyway. What followed were years of unspeakable abuse—years that nearly extinguished Sandy's will to remain on this earth at all.

I watched as the flood of images engulfed the room—disjointed fragments of memory, pain, and confusion bleeding into the air. It was as though his loneliness reached out, pulling all of us into its relentless gravity. When Sandy's projection finally faded, a dense, suffocating silence blanketed the room, heavy with the weight of what we had just witnessed. The air felt thick, as though no one dared to breathe. It was then that I noticed Lilith and Tomas had joined the group while Soren and I were away, now standing in human form for all to see.

The stillness was shattered when Soren suddenly stepped forward, startling everyone as he emerged from the shadows in his human guise, as if he had only just returned. The group jolted at his presence, and it dawned on me that, in their shock, none of them had even realized we were back.

"You really had it rough before we arrived, didn't you?" Soren said, his voice unusually soft, the words gentle, almost… compassionate.

The others stared, stunned. Soren's eyes were locked on Sandy, his gaze sharper than usual, yet oddly softened. "You're lucky Virgilian found you when he did," he continued, his tone almost kind. "Now, maybe you'll finally find your purpose."

Paisley scoffed, the sharpness of her voice cutting through the moment. "Look who's talking! You've been without purpose since before Earth even existed."

A slow, deliberate smirk spread across Soren's face. "Oh, how wrong you are," he murmured, his voice laced with dark amusement. "We all have a purpose now, don't we, boy?"

Before anyone could stop him, he reached out and placed a hand on Sandy's shoulder—his first real physical contact with the boy. Sandy froze, his body rigid, his eyes wide with fear. I felt a flash of alarm, half-expecting Soren to tighten his grip, to let his cruelty flare. But to my surprise, he didn't hurt him. He only stood there, his hand heavy but strangely gentle, a calculated intimacy that was more unnerving than any threat.

“Soren, leave the boy be,” I said, my voice steady, each word a careful warning. My movements were smooth, almost predatory, as I closed the distance, fixing my gaze on Sandy. With slow deliberation, I guided him away from Soren, a silent claim on his safety.

“It’s my turn now,” I continued, my tone casual but carrying an unmistakable weight. My eyes never left Sandy, my focus unwavering. “I’ll shape his mind into something we can use.” I projected a thought to him, a warning as sharp as a blade. He will hurt you if he can.

Sandy’s response came back with surprising confidence, He can’t hurt me with you near.

“Today is his day,” Virgilian declared, stepping forward to break the tension. “Since he’s finished sharing his short life, we’ll whisk him away on a grand adventure.”

Relief washed over me at Virgilian's words. A "grand adventure" sounded perfect—anything to get Sandy out of Soren's reach for a while, to let him breathe without the weight of Soren's scrutiny pressing down on him. I could finally relax, knowing he'd be close enough for me to intervene if anything went wrong, but far enough from Soren to feel safe.

I didn't watch them build the craft for Sandy's "great adventure day." I heard them, though—the sounds of muffled laughter, the occasional burst of excitement drifting up from below. Instead, I made myself comfortable on the roof, leaning back against the shingles and gazing up at the endless stretch of sky. I let myself feel distant, detached, as if I could pretend none of it mattered.

Out of the corner of my eye, I saw Soren slip away, crossing the yard and disappearing over to the neighbor's house. Something twisted in me, a flicker of unease sparking to life, whispering that no good would come from his presence there. But selfishly, I ignored it. Whatever trouble he was about to stir up over there, it was at least away from here—away from Sandy, away from me, and away from the fragile peace I'd carved out for myself on this rooftop.

I allowed myself the grim thought that whatever humans he was tormenting were a fair sacrifice for my own brief reprieve. It was hardly the first time. Let him take his games elsewhere, I thought, the words laced with bitterness and resignation. Let him find his pleasure in someone else's nightmares for once.
I tuned out the faint echoes of laughter and building below, and let myself drift into the silence. It was selfish comfort, yes, but right now, I didn't care.

□

Chapter Nine

Your electric guitar is one of my favorite creations. But you need to understand—it did not originate on Earth. Its origins lie far beyond your planet, on a world your kind could scarcely imagine. Seraphina has forbidden me from guiding you directly, so I can only nudge, only suggest in whispers and fragments. I cannot conjure instruments out of thin air and hand them to humans, nor can I teach your species to wield them outright. I must wait, patiently, until your kind is advanced enough to picture the impossible, to hear the music in their minds, and then craft it into something tangible.

The electric guitar, as you know it, traces its lineage to the distant planet of Tanbur—a world sculpted by the god Tabitha, the feminine counterpart to Tomas. It was a place of symphonies in motion, a planet brimming with sonic energy. Paisley, the creator of oceans, accelerated the evolution of life there, coaxing forth creatures of strength and resilience. Lilith, the divinity of awareness, took these beings and imbued them with self-reflection, the spark of soul. In less than a billion years, the inhabitants of Tanbur—tall, powerful creatures with skin like woven metal and ears attuned to the faintest tremor of sound—had achieved interplanetary travel. They became masters of vibration, manipulators of frequency. But their genius bore a dark side.

On Tanbur, the electric guitar was not born as a tool of art or joy. It was first conceived as an execution device. Their kind, with skin impenetrable to blades and bullets, could only be killed through their one weakness: their hypersensitive eardrums. A single, precise note, amplified and distorted, could rupture the mind and silence even the strongest among them. Thus, the electric guitar became the harbinger of death, a weapon that howled with both power and sorrow.

When I discovered this instrument, I was mesmerized. It fascinated me—not for its capacity to destroy, but for its potential to create. Its strings, its vibrations, its resonance... I saw in it the foundation of something extraordinary. I waited for the right moment, and when your Earth had ripened with ingenuity, I found my opportunity.

I whispered to two humans, dreamers both, a pair of Americans hungry for invention. They couldn’t know the origin of the idea I planted in their minds. They couldn’t know how the faint hum of inspiration came from me. I showed them visions of the guitar's form, nudged their imaginations toward its electric heart. I promised them it would change the world. And it did. What was once a weapon of execution became an instrument of expression, capable of shaking the air and stirring the soul.

So when you hold your electric guitar, when your fingers dance along its frets and its strings hum with the energy of your emotions, know this: you are playing something ancient, something reborn. An artifact of a distant galaxy, transformed by your kind into an object of beauty.

This was one of the many things I had been thinking about sharing with Sandy. When he arrived later that evening, slumped in the arms of Virgilian and Leopold as they carried him up the stairs like a limp child, I wondered if he would have the strength for our session. I had been brimming with ideas—new instruments, untapped musical foundations I was eager to introduce him to. But the sight of him drained and sagging in their arms tempered my excitement with concern.

As he settled under the covers, the yahudiyah convened once again. Despite his apparent slumber, we knew Sandy would hear us—and, as always, he would find a way to participate.

"I've never seen someone grow stronger and weaker at the same time," Virgilian remarked. His tone was grave, each word deliberate. "It's the most sensitive of subjects. I fear we're running out of time."

"Why don't we just cure him and kill him afterward?" Soren suggested flatly. The room grew taut with silence. Before any of us could muster a protest, Sandy's voice rang out, startlingly clear and sharp.

"Absolutely not," he projected from his bed, his words cutting through the air. "I am in no pain, and we still have plenty of time. Despite how I may appear, I am well."

"You won't be well for long if you don't let your mind rest," Paisley countered. "You are still human. Go to sleep—or I'll come up there and make sure you do."

"I am asleep," Sandy replied. His voice was calm but defiant. "My body is resting. My mind doesn't need this luxury anymore."

Virgilian shook his head, his frustration palpable even through the projection. "That brain of yours is still human, Sandy. It needs rest as much as the rest of you. Please, sleep. We need you at full strength tomorrow. We'll start again with two—just two—since we know you can handle non-human forms. But for now, sleep, or we'll continue without you."

For several moments, there was nothing but silence. Then the plan resumed, as though Sandy's absence from the conversation had been an agreement. It was decided: first me, then Paisley, would go next. My energy swelled with excitement at the certainty of my time with him. I had been waiting for this moment, cataloging all the things I wanted to share.

"When you've bored him to tears with your underwater universe that no one cares about," Soren interjected with his trademark smugness, "I'll step in to show him how hilariously flawed this universe is. I'll walk him through all the places evolution went off the rails and remind him why the Source should've intervened more often."

The thought made my thoughts twist, and not in a good way. The Source should have intervened long ago.
"Oh, goodie," Sandy projected suddenly, his tone laced with amusement. "Something from Soren to actually look forward to."

I froze. Sandy had heard everything. Not only that, he was willing to endure Soren's antics. I could hardly believe it.

"GO TO SLEEP!" we all shouted in unison, our voices converging into one collective command.

And finally, blessedly, Sandy obeyed. For the first time, the yahudiyah agreed to include Soren in the plan. When it was finally my turn, hours later, once Sandy was rested and strong enough, I insisted on being the one to intoxicate him. No one else would witness what transpired between us. I knew the effect he had on others after these sessions, and I wanted our encounter to remain private. If Soren caught even a whisper of what might unfold, the entire experiment could unravel. It would be over—done—and we might never know if it would have worked.

Sandy, now well-practiced in these rituals, nodded in agreement. His exhaustion showed, but his resolve to continue was unshaken. When he climbed into bed that evening, I took great care in intoxicating him, mirroring the delicate technique I had observed the others use. But as I touched his mind, I could feel his body in steep decline—the tumor eating away at him. It wouldn't be long now. Hours, maybe days, and this body would fail completely. That knowledge settled heavily on me, but I pushed it aside. I wasn't privileged to all the details about how this was supposed to work, and I didn't care. This would be my session, done my way.

As Sandy drifted into his trance, the boundaries of his reality began to blur. Colors melted into one another, shapes twisted and danced, and soon he was slipping into another realm. Slowly, he found himself standing in a vast, ethereal landscape—a place of swirling hues and dreamlike shapes, alive yet unknowable. I stepped forward, appearing beside him, fully materialized in my human form. My presence in his mind was both commanding and oddly gentle, designed to soothe and assert control simultaneously.

This was different from his previous sessions. The other Yahudiyah had shown him their memories as though he were an observer watching a film—distant and detached. But now, here I was, standing at his side, an active participant in his mind. I saw the way his defenses immediately rose, his stance stiffening as he instinctively assessed me for danger.

“Welcome,” I said softly, my voice carrying an almost musical cadence. “Here, we will explore the origins of music… and beyond.”

Sandy gave a curt nod, his expression wary but curious. I could see him working to suppress his unease, trying to extend me a tentative trust. Without waiting for further approval, I led him to a clearing where ancient instruments lay scattered on the ground. Each one pulsed faintly with light, as if alive, humming with energy. I knelt and picked up a lyre, its strings shimmering beneath my fingertips. As I began to play, the music unfolded around us, resonating deep within Sandy’s being, stirring memories and emotions buried long ago.

The melody wove through the air, conjuring visions in its wake. Sandy saw primitive beings striking stones together, discovering rhythm. He watched as the first crude instruments were crafted from bone and wood, their simple sounds evolving over time into something transcendent. Each note revealed a new chapter of music's history, weaving a tapestry of its evolution and its profound connection to life itself.

Sandy stood transfixed, his face softening as he began to absorb the depth of what I was showing him. He felt the rhythms awaken something dormant inside him, an ancient connection to the origins of sound and expression. My music drew him deeper into the narrative, unveiling how melodies had been used to heal, to communicate, to unify. It was more than the birth of music—it was the story of humanity's soul, laid bare in song.

"Music is more than sound," I explained as my fingers danced across the lyre's strings. "It is the language of the soul. A bridge between worlds."

As I played, the visions grew richer. Sandy saw shamans pounding drums to mend broken spirits, bards singing heroic epics to keep history alive, orchestras moving audiences to tears with their harmonies. The sheer power of music unfolded before him, undeniable and overwhelming.

But something shifted. I noticed the tension returning to Sandy's stance, his eyes darting away from the images I was showing him. He was searching for something more—something I hadn't offered.

"Why are you only showing me this?" Sandy asked, his voice calm but laced with curiosity—and suspicion. "What are you hiding?"

My fingers stilled on the lyre. I met his gaze, the music fading into the stillness between us. I wanted to lie, to deflect, but his question struck a chord too deep to ignore.

"What I show you is what you need to see," I replied carefully. But the resolve in Sandy's eyes told me he wasn't satisfied.

The world around us shifted without warning. We stood now in a grand hall, its polished wood floors gleaming beneath crystal chandeliers. A symphony filled the space, music cascading from every corner. Sandy glanced down and gasped as he realized he was no longer himself—he had become a violin. He felt the bow sliding across his strings, each stroke coaxing out notes that resonated in his soul. The prodigy child playing him had no sheet music—only the raw flow of inspiration, channeling something beyond human comprehension.

But even amidst the beauty of this moment, Sandy's mind reached outward, pushing beyond the confines of what I had crafted for him. And then, to my shock, he did something no human had ever done: he took control.

I felt it instantly—his presence, invasive and strong, diving into the recesses of my mind. He reached past the barriers I had erected, prying at memories I had buried deep. For a fleeting moment, he glimpsed a vision I hadn't meant to share: Soren, monstrous and towering, standing in a field littered with the bodies of lifeless creatures. Their glassy eyes stared into oblivion as storm clouds churned above. The image was violent and raw, and as soon as I felt him see it, I slammed the door shut, forcefully expelling him from my mind.

Sandy gasped as he returned to his body, trembling in his bed, his eyes wide with accusation. He stared at me, his face etched with betrayal. I felt my anger rise, sharp and immediate.

"How dare you?" I snarled, my voice trembling with fury. "I could destroy you in an instant. Why would you tempt my wrath?"

"You're wasting my time," Sandy shot back, his tone biting. "Why hide what we both know is there? Soren is a monster—fine. But I need to know how you stand beside him. Show me!"

My anger simmered, but I refused to give him what he wanted. "You'll see Soren through his perspective, not mine," I said coldly. "You will take what I give you, and no more."

Sandy's laugh was bitter and dismissive. "I've had enough," he said sharply. "I've learned your tricks, your remarkable ability to stand still for centuries and ignore what's right in front of you. Thanks for that."

He tore himself free from my influence, severing the connection with a finality that left me reeling. Stunned, my fury ignited, boiling over into something raw and uncontrollable. Blinded by vengeance, I fell back on instinct—on what I always did when this kind of rage consumed me: I summoned Soren.

Reaching out with all my energy, I sought him wherever he might be. Luckily, he wasn't far—next door, of course, tormenting the neighbors in his usual fashion. He arrived instantly, his dark, oppressive presence spilling into the room like a storm. Without hesitation, he plunged into Sandy's mind, his suffocating force wrapping around it like an unrelenting vise.

The onslaught was immediate—memories, thoughts, and emotions flooding Sandy's consciousness at a speed no human could endure. His mind fractured under the weight of Soren's vast, chaotic existence. I stood frozen, horrified at what I had unleashed.

It wasn't until Virgilian appeared, summoned by Sandy's silent distress, that the storm finally subsided. With practiced precision, Virgilian erected a mental barrier, shielding Sandy from further harm. As Sandy gasped for air, his body convulsing violently, Virgilian turned to me, his gaze piercing.

He didn't have to say it—I already knew. This was my fault. The weight of that realization pinned me in place, my limbs frozen as if I'd forgotten how to move. Pailey swept into the room with her usual calm, focused energy, wasting no time as she began the delicate work of mending the boy's fractured mind.

My energy constricted, fear knotting tighter with every second. What if it was too late? What if the damage I had caused couldn't be undone? The thought clawed at me relentlessly: This is my fault.

From the corner of my eye, I caught Lilith and Tomas watching. Their gaze shifted between Pailey's efforts and me, their expressions unreadable but heavy with judgment. I didn't need words from them to feel it—I could feel their condemnation like a weight pressing down on me.

It wasn't the first time someone I cared about had been hurt by Soren, but this time, the weight of responsibility clung to me like a shadow I couldn't outrun. The blame was inescapable, gnawing at the edges of my mind.

Before I could sink too deeply into my thoughts, Soren turned to me. His presence was oppressive, his voice cutting through the silence—low, sharp, and commanding.
"Follow me."

Without waiting for my reply, he moved to the window, and I followed. We slipped through the frame and dissolved into the wind, our forms blending with the swirling night air.

"You're all wrong," Soren said, his voice fierce and insistent as it carried on the breeze. "It's not the boy—it's Sarah Francis." He glanced at me, his eyes sharp, burning with purpose. "Remind yourself of creation—of her already in existence. Do you not see it? She was there, long before any of the others."
My mind was elsewhere, still on Sandy, his suffering like a weight pressing down on me. Soren's ravings about Sarah Francis barely registered. His words felt distant, muffled against the roar of my guilt.

"I see her with the rest of us," I projected to him finally. "She was there, yes, but not before us."

"No!" Soren's rage flared, the energy crackling around him like a storm. "She was there first! We are not the first children of the Source—she is."

I stayed silent, my thoughts tangled in Sandy's pain and my role in it. And then there was Paganini—what I had allowed to happen, what I had ignored because I selfishly enjoyed the music we created. The guilt was suffocating.

"I hope the boy survives what we've done to him," I said softly, the words heavy with regret.

Soren's fury spiked, his energy swirling dangerously around us. Why does no one care about this but me?! His voice thundered in my mind, vibrating with frustration. "The boy is irrelevant. Sarah Francis is the key, and no one is listening! Why must I prove this to you?"

I held steady, letting his storm rage around me. I didn't respond, and the silence between us became a tangible thing—dense, charged, and dangerous.

“I’ll prove it, then,” Soren said, his voice quiet but laced with determination. He drew me into a wind pocket, the currents carrying us swiftly through the skies.

Crossing the oceans once more, we returned to the side of the planet we preferred. But to my surprise, he didn’t take me back to Austria as I had expected. Instead, we drifted south, gliding over the jagged peaks of the Alps and into the sun-soaked expanse of Italy. I didn’t ask where we were going, it didn’t matter. The guilt of what I had done had hollowed me out, dulling every thought, every feeling.

I followed him without question, not because I trusted him, but because I had no will left to decide anything for myself.

We arrived at a sleek apartment building in Milan, its facade glistening with understated wealth. I sensed something strange—the building was almost completely void of life. Only one human was inside. It was odd. This wasn’t an abandoned relic; it was a place for the elite, yet it felt deserted.

Soren moved with purpose, leading me directly to that single presence. Without ceremony, he materialized in a dimly lit kitchen, where a man sat at the table, calmly eating a sandwich. The moment the man saw us, he froze. His eyes widened in recognition, and then, trembling, he dropped to his knees, his hands shaking as though in reverence.

"Thank you, my lord Soren," the man whispered, his voice trembling with awe and reverence, as though each word were a sacred offering. "Thank you for pushing me beyond my small desires. I would never have thought so big without you. It worked—better than I could have imagined."

The man's face gleamed with a twisted pride, his lips curling into a smile that didn't quite reach his haunted eyes. "I framed the neighbor, just like I planned," he continued, his voice quickening with excitement, "but with your guidance… it became so much more. The family is gone now. Completely wiped out. I have their fortune, their property, everything. It's all mine to do with as I please." He exhaled sharply, as though reveling in the enormity of his own crime.

I studied him, disgust coiling deep within me. The man's boast was nothing new to me—just another disciple in a long, unbroken chain of men who had pledged their loyalty to Soren across thousands of years. Always the same: vile, wretched creatures who believed that acts of cruelty committed in his name would somehow please him. They thought themselves chosen. Special. But they were nothing more than puppets, swayed by Soren's honeyed lies and promises of power.

I was never happy to see one of them, and Soren knew it.

The man's feverish voice cut through my thoughts. "Now that I have the family's wealth, the building will be mine soon enough. The papers are almost ready. No one will ever question what happened to them. Not after the trail I left behind." He grinned, sharp and wolfish, a predator drunk on his kill.

That was when the smell hit me.

It crept into my senses, faint at first, then suffocating: the cloying, metallic tang of blood, laced with the unmistakable stench of decay. It wasn't just one body. This man was steeped in death. He had bathed in someone's blood, not long ago. My gut churned as the full weight of it hit me—there had been many victims. Too many to count. Their presence clung to him like a shadow, a sinister aura that seemed to pulse in the air around him.

Soren tilted his head, a faint smile playing on his lips. "Matteo," he said, his voice silken, laced with dark amusement. "Allow me to introduce you to your mother."

"I am not his mother," I said evenly, my voice a cool blade against the tension in the room. materialize beside him, my form sharpening from the mist until I stood solid and human-like My eyes locked onto Matteo, cold and unyielding. "Don't kneel to me."

Matteo dropped to his knees anyway, his hands pressed together in trembling reverence. His lips moved in silent prayer, his gaze darting between me and Soren like a devout before a pair of gods.

"Oh, but you are his mother," Soren said, a dark grin curling his mouth. "Just as much as I am his father. You shaped him as surely as I did." His eyes flicked to me, probing, taunting. "You can deny it all you like, but he is yours. Ours."

I met his gaze without flinching. "I will not lay claim to this… person," I said, my tone colder than the void between stars. "He is no child of mine."

Soren's grin faded, his expression hardening. "Are you not my mate?" he asked sharply, a quiet venom in his voice.

"I am," I answered, my voice flat, almost disinterested. I had long since learned not to react to his provocations. But I could sense where this was going, and it churned something uneasy in my chest.

"Then he is our child," Soren pressed, his tone sharpening with accusation. "You cannot simply cast off your part in this. You allowed me to create children like him. You allowed this—just as you've allowed so many other things."

"I will not," I said, each word deliberate, pointed. "You breed your cruel bastards on a whim. I have no control over what you choose to do, no say in the bloodlines you corrupt."

His eyes narrowed. "No control? No say? You think your indifference absolves you?" He leaned closer, his voice softening, almost tender. "My bastards exist because of you. Every single one of them is born from the space you leave for me, from the distance you've always kept between us. You permit this, even if you deny it."

His words were like ice, slipping beneath my soul, but I didn't let him see the cracks they made. Instead, I turned my gaze away, my expression unreadable. His obsession with Sarah Francis, had done nothing to lessen the weight of my guilt. If anything, it only deepened it, forcing me to question the ways Soren's corruption had seeped into me, tainting everything I touched. Was it possible I had become complicit without even realizing it? Had his evil transferred to me as surely as it had to his followers?

Soren's voice interrupted my thoughts, now calm, cold, and full of authority. "If you need proof, then proof you shall have."

He turned to Matteo, who was still on his knees, trembling like a dog awaiting its master's command.

"You have a car, I assume?" Soren asked smoothly.

"Y-yes, my lord," Matteo stammered, scrambling to his feet. He moved with frantic energy, gathering his things with shaking hands. "I'll drive you anywhere. Anywhere you wish."

"Good," Soren said, his eyes gleaming with dark intent. "Then lead the way."

Minutes later, we followed Matteo to a dimly lit parking garage, the stale air heavy with the distant hum of traffic above. He opened the door to an expensive car—sleek, black, and polished to a shine—and slid into the driver's seat, his fingers fumbling over the ignition.

"I await your instructions, my lord," Matteo said, his voice reverent as he gripped the steering wheel.
Soren leaned forward, his expression sharp with cruel amusement. "Austria," he said simply. "I want to show you where your real parents live."

□

Chapter Ten

The drive stretched on for hours, the road unfolding endlessly under the faint glow of passing headlights. Matteo was occasionally allowed to stop—brief respites to refuel the car, grab a bite to eat, or relieve himself—but rest, true rest, was out of the question. Soren saw to that. His voice carried an unspoken command: Matteo would not sleep until they reached their destination. Exhaustion clung to the man like a second skin, but his fervor, his blind devotion to Soren, burned brighter than any fatigue.

As the car hummed along, I allowed myself a rare indulgence: the quiet pleasure of the ride. There was something deeply soothing about the steady rhythm of the tires meeting the road, a physical connection to the world that I found grounding. Few things brought me solace these days, but the sensation of moving forward—of motion itself—allowed me to momentarily unburden my mind. I leaned back against the seat and let the vibrations of the car ripple through me, focusing on nothing but the way the road rolled beneath us.

For a while, I succeeded in pushing everything else away. I let my thoughts rest, brushing aside the ever-present guilt tied to Sandy, the tangled knot of my relationship with Soren, and the weight of my past. I let it all slip into the shadows of my mind, sinking into the kind of stillness I had once mastered during the times I pretended to be nothing more than an instrument. Even as the physical world moved around me, I felt an emptiness take hold within—a practiced nothingness, a void where emotions and memories were quieted.

But not completely.

I already knew where we were going. The destination was etched into my very being, a place I could not forget, even if I wanted to.

Enns.

Nestled in the heart of Upper Austria, Enns is one of the oldest towns in the region, a settlement whose history reaches back to the time of the Romans, when it bore the name Lauriacum. Archaeologists might speak of its Roman military camp and the thriving civilian town that blossomed in the first century, but they would never find what truly lies beneath. This land, older than the Empire, is steeped in myths far more ancient. It has always been a place of power, long before humans claimed it, long before the soil bore their footprints.

Unlike Virgilian, who buried himself in the solitude of a mountain cave, or Lilith and Tomas, who carved out their hidden city beneath the dark belly of the Russian earth, Soren and I chose to walk openly under the sun. For centuries, we lived here, among the people. They knew us then, revered us. But as the years passed, and human memories began to shift and fade, it became necessary to withdraw. We stopped appearing before them, retreating into the background, but we never truly left.

To us, Enns was more than a settlement. It was ours—a piece of the world we had claimed together. The soil itself seemed to hum with familiarity, as if it remembered the press of our feet, the weight of our presence. Each iteration of the town, each building constructed on the bones of the old, was a continuation of that home. It was a place that knew us, as deeply as we knew it.

Our first stop was a sprawling estate on the outskirts of town, its silhouette stark against the deepening night. The structure, though weathered by centuries, still stood tall and proud, its essence preserved by my will.
"This was once our home," Soren said to Matteo, his voice laced with nostalgia. "Your mother and I built it over a thousand years ago. It still stands because she has willed it so."

I stood in silence, staring at the estate, my expression unreadable. Matteo glanced at me, searching for some sign of recognition, but I gave him none. I had spent centuries tending to this place, returning when the town needed protection, discreetly funneling funds and materials to ensure its survival. I had been its silent guardian, an angel they never knew existed. Yet standing here now, with Matteo's expectant gaze upon me, I felt nothing but an old weariness.

"I am not his kin," I said flatly, breaking the silence. I turned to Matteo, my gaze sharp and unyielding. "Unlike the masculine Yahudiyah, the feminine cannot reproduce in human form. We don't know why. So, no, we are not related. You are the spawn of one of the many bastards he sired during our time as husband and wife—when I could not give him children."

Matteo's face shifted, a flicker of confusion breaking through his reverence. Before he could speak, I turned to Soren, my voice cutting through the stillness. "Why are we here, Soren?"

Soren smiled faintly, a shadow of something unreadable crossing his face. "I want our child to see where we first tried."

"Tried what?" Matteo asked, his voice tentative.

"Tried to build some sort of human legacy," Soren replied, his tone tinged with an almost bitter amusement.

"That was never my intention," I said, my voice cold as frost. "I never wanted a legacy. I only wanted to know what it felt like to be human."

Matteo looked at me, curiosity lighting his tired eyes. "How is it different from being you?"

"It is different in every way," I replied simply. And yet, in the back of my mind, a quiet thought lingered: Or at least it used to be. I had lived too many human lives now, taken on too much of their fragile nature. "You are mostly physical," I continued. "Very little of you is spirit. We, on the other hand, are mostly spirit and barely physical. The emotions you experience—the feelings that drive you—were impossible for us before we lived among you. We didn't understand them."

"Exactly," Soren interjected. His voice had taken on a new tone, softer yet edged with a deeper intensity. "Before that first human life, I had never felt that parent-like connection to anyone or anything outside the Source—until my first human mother." He paused, his eyes distant, as though looking back through time. "Do you remember her? Growing inside her body, being cradled in her love. That sense of doing right, simply by existing in her presence—it was something I had never known. Not before her, and not since her death… until Sarah Francis."

I stiffened. His fascination with Sarah Francis was beginning to gnaw at me. He spoke of her as though she had redeemed him, but I had seen the truth of his behavior. He wasn't redeemed. He hadn't changed. He was the same creature who tormented Sandy's neighbors, the same being who had left chaos in his wake time and time again.

"It's not Sarah Francis," I said coolly. "Just as it wasn't your human mother. This time, it's the boy. Last time, it was human trauma." My gaze hardened. "Take him. Show him what you became after she was gone."
Soren's eyes flicked toward me, but he said nothing. At my insistence, we climbed back into the car and drove into town. The estate, with its memories and its ghosts, faded into the night behind us.

He took us to the center of Enns, where the Stadtturm—the Enns Tower—stood tall and resolute, a sentinel overlooking the heart of the town square. Its Renaissance architecture was a proud relic of history, its stone walls rising high against the evening sky, its clock ticking away the hours for generations of townsfolk who walked beneath its shadow without ever knowing the secrets it held. To them, it was simply a tower, a monument to their ancestors' ambition and autonomy. They had no idea that this tower was far more than a symbol of the past—it was a fortress of hidden truths.

Construction of the tower had begun in 1564, commissioned by the city council to serve as both a watchtower and a clock tower, its spire a mark of the town's wealth and independence. But those were merely surface-level purposes. The true design, the unseen intentions behind its construction, were Soren's doing. His whispers had guided the architects' hands, his influence shaping the foundation, the walls, the very stones. It was completed in 1568, and when the final brick was laid, Soren silenced the workers forever. I remembered it vividly—the quiet way he dispatched them, ensuring that no mortal would ever speak of the hidden chamber carved into the heart of the tower.

It had been our sanctuary once. A secret refuge hidden behind layers of stone and time, untouched by mortal eyes. Time had barely touched it either, though now it was heavy with the scent of dust and the slow decay of abandonment. Neither of us had walked these halls in years.

We pulled up just outside the square and approached the tower. The bustling life of the town faded as we rounded to a small, inconspicuous door at the tower's base, unnoticed by the townsfolk who hurried past. Soren moved with calm precision, his energy shifting imperceptibly until it shaped itself into the form of a key. It slid smoothly into the ancient lock. The door creaked open, revealing a narrow, dimly lit passageway.

Soren entered first, striding forward with a practiced ease, his familiarity with the space as strong as if no time had passed. He stopped midway down the hall, his hand brushing against the cold stone wall. With a deliberate motion, he pressed a hidden panel, and the wall shifted with a low groan, revealing a concealed staircase spiraling downward.

I lingered, watching Matteo's wide eyes take in the secret passage. His breath quickened, his reverence for Soren momentarily tempered by the weight of the place. I didn't speak, but my memory filled the silence. I could still see the faces of the men Soren had killed here, the ones who had built the tower and sealed its secrets. He had murdered them to protect this place, to erase any trace of what lay below. This was his way: cruelty justified by necessity.

The stairs descended into shadow, and as we followed, the air grew cooler, heavier, thick with the echoes of old memories. At the bottom, the passage opened into the dungeon—a vast, oppressive space that felt frozen in time. Dust hung in the air like a shroud, clinging to every surface. The faint scurry of small creatures fled at our arrival, and the faint glow of our forms illuminated the room, casting eerie shadows on the walls.

The instruments of cruelty still lay where they had been left, their edges dulled by disuse but their purpose clear. Chains hung from the walls, and tables stained with ancient, rust-colored streaks bore the marks of past torment. I felt a wave of unease settle over me as I took it all in. This was not just a room—it was a monument to Soren's darkness, to the worst parts of himself unleashed.

"This," I said, my voice cold and edged with disdain, "is what he became. He used her death as an excuse to unleash the unspeakable."

Soren stepped forward, brushing the dust from a table with his hand, his expression unreadable. "When she died," he said softly, "I was finally free to be myself again."

"You've always been yourself," I countered sharply. "No one could limit your self-expression if they wanted to."

"You're wrong," Soren replied, his gaze fixed on the room. Matteo wandered cautiously among the relics, his movements tentative, as if afraid to disturb the past. Soren's voice darkened as he continued, "While she lived, I found it hard to truly be me. Hard to disappoint her. One look from her—just one—and she could stop me. Freeze me in place. I don't think you've ever understood that kind of power."

I scoffed, folding my arms. "No, Soren. What I understand is that you are no one's prisoner but your own. You've always been free."

Soren ignored me, his tone turning distant, haunted. "Until the day she was taken from me, there was nothing I wouldn't do to please her. And then the soldiers..." His voice faltered for the briefest moment, then turned cold as ice. "The Romans."

My gaze flickered at the mention of them. "Yes. The Romans."

"In my weak form, I killed thirty-seven of them that day," Soren said quietly, almost detached. His eyes met mine, and for a moment, the faintest trace of something like guilt crossed his face. "And I killed you too," he added, his voice lower still.

My stomach twisted, though my expression remained cold. "Yes," I said sharply. "You killed me too. Did that make you feel free, Soren? Did that ease your chains?"

His gaze darkened, unreadable. "Would you have preferred what they did to my mother?" he asked, his voice low and biting.

I stepped closer, my words cutting like steel. "I didn't have the luxury of deciding. You murdered me before I even had the chance to choose."

His jaw tightened. "I spared you," he insisted.

"No," I said, my voice like ice. "You spared yourself."

For a moment, silence filled the room, heavy with unspoken accusations and buried truths. Then Soren turned his back to me, his eyes sweeping over the dungeon. "The reason we're here," he began, his voice steady but tense, "is this. I needed to return—to feel it again, what I've only ever felt in this place." He paused, his gaze drifting as if the past still hung in the air. "It's a feeling I can't fully explain—a resistance to the darkness. A pull away from what I am. I only ever felt it when she was near."

"And now…" His voice faltered, the words dragging as though weighed down by something he couldn't quite name. "I feel the same restraint. It's like an invisible hand holding me back, something I can't break free from, something that stops me from disappointing her—even in death." He exhaled slowly, his brow furrowed, his expression caught somewhere between confusion and vulnerability. "I feel it again when I'm near Sarah Francis. The same… inability. The same pull away from what I am."

His words hung in the air, heavy with unspoken desperation. He was pleading—begging me to understand—but I couldn't. I didn't feel it. Whatever invisible force he claimed tethered him to Sarah Francis, whatever resistance he swore she awakened in him, it was utterly alien to me. If such a thing existed, I was blind to it. I couldn't see the invisible hand. I couldn't feel the restraint.

What his deranged speech stirred in me instead was something entirely different: the memory of Viviana and Leland.

The thought slipped unbidden into my mind, sharp and intrusive. Perhaps it was his mention of Sarah Francis, or perhaps it was the raw, aching need in his voice—the way he sought connection, sought meaning—that made me think of them. Viviana and Leland, the couple who had been one since the moment of their creation, who had existed as a single, unbreakable unit, indivisible in spirit. And yet, against all logic, all nature, they had split.

I could never understand how that had been possible. How could something created as one be torn apart? The very thought of it had unsettled me, but now it loomed large in my mind. As Soren rambled about Sarah Francis and his supposed redemption, I found myself wondering if something similar had happened to us. If there had once been a unity between Soren and me that had since fractured into something irreparable.

How could we have split?

I stared at him as he spoke, his voice unsteady, full of a strange and unfamiliar longing. I wanted to feel something for him in that moment, to feel some connection to the weight of his words. But all I felt was the echo of Viviana and Leland, the ghost of something broken and far beyond repair.

After more futile attempts on his part to explain something that refused to register in my mind, I realized the gulf between us was growing. He didn't see it. He couldn't see it. The feelings he described—the restraint, the pull—they didn't come from Sarah Francis. They came from two places: the curse of living human lives and the one constant that had survived us all—Sandy. The boy was the key. He had endured everything we had thrown at him, everything the universe had wrought, and he was still alive. I could feel him, his presence tugging at the edges of my consciousness like a faint, insistent whisper. I could almost hear him calling me, even across time and space.

Soren needed to understand this. He had to see it for what it was.

"Stop," I commanded, my voice sharp and cutting through the rising tension. His words halted midstream, and the room seemed to grow still around us. "I need you to listen, Soren. You were different because being human brought you emotions. New, overwhelming feelings that came with the weight of flesh and blood. We weren't ready for that. None of us were." I paused, searching his face for any flicker of understanding. "Lilith never warned us. She never told us what human lives would do to us, how they would change us. It's not Sarah Francis, Soren! Why can't you see it? The changes you're feeling—they're because of the boy!" Soren's expression darkened, his jaw tightening as his eyes bore into mine. "Fine," he said, his voice low and simmering with barely contained frustration. Before I could react, he moved.

Faster than thought, he transformed. His hands gripped me with a strength that was no longer human, his inhuman swiftness carrying us up the spiraling stairs before Matteo could even register what was happening. The passageway sealed behind us as though it had never been opened, locking Matteo below. It hadn't been intentional—just Soren moving too quickly for anyone else to keep up—but the realization settled uneasily in my chest. Matteo was a monster, yes, but he didn't deserve to die abandoned in that basement.

Or maybe he did.

I pushed the thought aside, unwilling to confront it now. What I knew for certain was this: I didn't want to feel responsible for another human death—not because of my inaction, not because I couldn't muster the effort to save them.

"You can't just leave him down there!" I protested as we emerged into the night air. The chill hit me like a slap, but Soren was already moving, his strides unrelenting.

He didn’t even glance back. "I’m going to prove to you that it’s Sarah Francis, not the boy," he said, his tone cold and unyielding.

I opened my mouth to argue further, but something in his expression made me hesitate. There was a wildness in his eyes, a determination that bordered on desperation. I didn’t trust it, but I followed him anyway. I had no choice.

He led me through the winding streets of Enns with purpose, his eyes scanning the surroundings like a predator searching for prey. I didn’t know what he was looking for—until he stopped abruptly.

A church.

The first one he saw, he entered.

The heavy wooden doors creaked as Soren pushed them open, the sound reverberating through the quiet, cavernous space. Inside, the building was dim and still, the faint scent of incense lingering in the air. The flickering light of a few candles illuminated the stone walls, their glow casting long, wavering shadows. The emptiness was palpable, the silence broken only by the faint rustle of cloth as Soren moved toward the pews.

He knew exactly what he would find.

There, near the front of the sanctuary, sat a lone figure—a frail, elderly man, his shoulders bowed in silent prayer. His lips moved in rhythm with the whispered words of his devotion, his focus wholly on whatever plea he was offering to the heavens. He didn't notice our approach, not until it was far too late.

In an instant, Soren shed his human guise, his form unraveling into its true, terrifying essence. He became a swirling mass of energy, crimson lightning crackling through the air, casting jagged shadows against the church walls. The transformation sent a wave of electric pressure through the room, making the very air feel heavier, harder to breathe.

The old man froze mid-prayer, his hands gripping the pew in front of him as terror locked his frail body in place. His wide, disbelieving eyes met Soren's storm-like form. Before he could scream—or even utter a prayer for protection—Soren moved, his power surging forward with predatory intent.

He invaded the man's body like smoke pouring into an open window, forcing his essence into the man's nostrils and down his throat. The man's chest heaved, his back arching as he was made to inhale deeply, helpless against the surge of unnatural energy overtaking him. Moments later, his body went slack, collapsing against the pew as if sedated by Soren's overwhelming presence.

Soren leaned close, his form a burning aura around the man's still body, his thoughts projecting directly into the man's trembling mind. "I am Soren," he said, his voice reverberating through the man's consciousness like the tolling of a funeral bell. "One of the first children of the Source. You carry a fragment of it within you—watching all you do but never intervening. These are your final moments on this world. I need you to understand who your creator truly is. Do you understand me?"

The man, half-dazed and wide-eyed with terror, gave a weak, trembling nod. His breath came in shallow, labored gasps, his spirit already teetering on the edge of departure.

Without hesitation, Soren's energy surged forward again, this time reaching into the man's body like a shadow made flesh. In one swift, brutal motion, he severed the man's organs from their places. The death was instant—merciful, perhaps, in its efficiency, though mercy had nothing to do with it.

The man's soul slipped free of its mortal shell, luminous and pulsing with a strength that startled even me. Soren caught it as it fled, gripping the fragile essence tightly as it tried to escape. And then, without warning, he turned to me, his power unfurling in a wave that engulfed me, wrapping me in his energy.

Before I could protest, we were pulled violently upward, our essences tearing through the cracks in the church's walls, hurtling skyward with impossible speed. The sensation was jarring, like being ripped from my body and flung into the cosmos. As we ascended, I could feel the old man's soul radiating with the purity of a faithful life. His spirit pulsed with strength, and though I was repulsed by Soren's act, I couldn't ignore the intoxicating rush he felt from it.

I knew what awaited him. The Wall.

But this time was different.

As we approached the Wall, Soren released me just before impact. He still had enough presence of mind, enough control, to spare me the brunt of what was coming. I was cast aside, left hovering in the space just beyond it, watching as he collided head-on. The impact was violent, brutal. He writhed against the invisible force, his essence searing with pain as the Wall rejected him. The agony was immense, washing over him in waves, his form flickering like a flame caught in a windstorm.

I stayed by his side, as I always did, helping him weather the storm. To my surprise, however, the suffering lasted only hours, not the days or weeks I had expected. When he finally peeled himself away from the Wall, free of its torment, he steadied himself, his form regaining its usual shape.

“See?” he said, his voice calm now, almost triumphant.

I narrowed my eyes, my tone sharp. “What am I supposed to see?” I demanded. “Yes, the pain passed quickly this time, but we don’t know anything about that man. You don’t know what kind of life he led. For all we know, he could’ve been in that church to steal.”

I shook my head, incredulous. “And you’re impressed by this? We’ve seen this before, Soren. Sometimes the withdrawal is unbearable, and sometimes we get lucky. This was luck, nothing more.”

His satisfaction soured into anger at my words. His form trembled, his energy darkening with frustration. Without a word, he dove, plummeting from the sky like a needle slicing through the clouds. His descent was violent, reckless, a testament to the rage boiling within him.

This time, I didn’t follow. I hovered there, watching as he spiraled downward, out of control. For the first time in what felt like an eternity, I let him go.

Instead, I returned to Austria, to the tower where we had left Matteo. The air was thick with the weight of Soren's absence as I approached the door. Without hesitation, I opened it, leaving it ajar for Matteo to free himself. I didn't check to see if he emerged alive or unscathed. I didn't care. I had done my part in sparing his life; the rest was up to him.

From there, I returned to the only place I still found peace—my museum. The halls were alive with the quiet hum of preparation, the staff busy cleaning and arranging displays for an upcoming exhibition. Their movements were methodical, oblivious to my presence. I passed by them without a word, making my way to Mozart's piano, an anchor in a world that had grown increasingly unmoored.

For the first time in decades, I materialized into my human form in plain sight, unconcerned with who might see. The effort of hiding no longer mattered. I sat before the piano and placed my hands on the keys, the cool ivory smooth beneath my fingertips.

And then, I played.

The music poured from me, raw and unrestrained, echoing through the quiet halls. The staff stopped their work, their eyes wide as they gathered to watch. For hours, I played, pouring every thought, every feeling, every ounce of my being into the notes. My private audience stood enraptured, bearing witness to what might have been my greatest performance.

In those hours, the world felt distant. And for a brief, fleeting moment, I remembered what it felt like to be at peace.

□

Chapter Eleven

I felt him enter my space the moment his energy breached the museum's walls. It pulsed like a gathering storm, sharp and electric, sending ripples through the air. I didn't need to see him to know he was here. I felt him in the fibers of the building itself, in the way the atmosphere shifted and grew taut with his presence.

There I was, playing my favorite piano in my own museum, my form an otherworldly swirl of cloud, dust, and garnet-hued energy. The workers had sealed the doors hours ago, keeping the outside world at bay, trapped within the strange phenomenon unfolding before their eyes. They couldn't leave even if they wanted to. My haunting performance had captivated them, my fingers of light and dust dancing over the ivory keys, creating a melody that felt like it stretched through time itself. But I hadn't played for them. I hadn't played for anyone. I played purely for myself, the sound spilling from me like a confession, raw and unrestrained.

And then Soren came.

He entered the room like the wrath of nature itself, his energy crackling red-hot as lightning arced across the room. The air warped around him, shimmering with his raw power. The workers barely had time to gasp before the first strike hit. Blood-red lightning lashed out, tearing through the air and striking every human in the room. They fell like puppets with their strings cut, lifeless before their bodies hit the floor.

All but one.

I froze, horror spreading through me like ice. It was my fault. Again. I hadn't meant for this to happen, but deep down, I knew I had drawn him here. Had I not come, had I found somewhere isolated to exist, they would still be alive. I had condemned them without meaning to.

Soren's focus shifted to the lone survivor, who now cowered on the floor, trembling, his breath coming in ragged, terrified gasps. Soren moved with swift, unrelenting precision. His energy wrapped around the man like a vice, tightening until the air itself seemed to quake under the strain. The man's pleas for mercy went unheard; Soren's attention was locked on me.

"Our time here is done," he said, his voice low and crackling, vibrating in the charged air. "Follow me, and I will prove it."

Before I could respond, Soren turned back to the survivor, fixing him with an unrelenting gaze. His voice was calm, almost tender, as he said, "You are number eight. What you need to know is this: the source of all things lives within you. When you die, the tiny piece of the source, fractured and scattered, will return to its creator. I am that creator's first child."

And then, with effortless cruelty, he tore the man's soul from his body. It was not gentle. The man's spirit wrenched free with a silent, luminous scream, trembling and quivering as the last fragile traces of his humanity clung to it. His body crumpled to the floor, lifeless, discarded like an empty husk—forgotten in an instant.

Soren surged forward, seizing the soul with the ferocity of a hunter claiming its prey. He rode it like a blazing comet, its light dimming under his dominion, and I had no choice but to follow, dragged along in his wake.
I followed, entwining my essence with his as we raced toward the wall that had long defined the limits of our existence. At the last moment, I let go, watching as he collided with the wall head-on. The impact was brutal, the force rippling outward in a wave that cracked against the fabric of reality itself. But this time, Soren didn't falter.

He hit the wall, and though pain flickered across his face, it passed almost instantly. His form didn't waver, didn't break. He remained hovering, whole and unbroken, his energy stabilizing as though the agony of the wall had no hold on him anymore.

I watched him, my own essence trembling with unease. He had wanted me to see this, to understand what he had learned. And I did. He had built a tolerance. The wall—the pain, the withdrawal, the searing torment—no longer had power over him.

Soren turned to me, projecting his thoughts directly into my mind. His voice resonated with a calm certainty that unsettled me.
"The suffering can be conquered," he said. "After thousands of years, I've built a resistance in days. The wall—its pain—it was never real. It was always in our minds." His gaze locked onto mine, unwavering and intense. "So, what else is all in our minds? What else have we believed without questioning?"

My expression tightened. I could barely keep the strain out of my voice. "I've lost the ability to understand you," I said coldly. "You're… you're past reason, Soren. You're not the person I knew anymore. You're a stranger to me."

He moved closer, his gaze filled with a wild, unsettling urgency. "You're wrong," he said. "I've found clarity. I'm telling you—there are things we can see now, things that have always been there but we couldn't perceive before. The reason we can see them now is because she wants us to. Don't you see? You just have to look."

I shook my head, my tone sharp with frustration. "I don't know if we're seeing the same things, Soren. What I see is the boy—Sandy. Why can't you see it's him? Why can't you accept that a human has earned my trust? Everyone's trust except yours."

Soren's expression darkened, his energy flaring briefly before settling into something cold and controlled. "Then I will show you," he said, his voice disturbingly calm. "I will show everyone."

Without waiting for my response, he turned and tore through the air, crossing oceans with an urgency that felt almost manic. I followed reluctantly, unable to shake the growing weight of unease in my chest. After hours of silence, we arrived in Jacksonville. Soren moved with purpose through the narrow streets, his attention focused on something I couldn't see—until I did.

A lone figure emerged from a nearby church: a man, unassuming and unaware of what was coming. Soren's energy gleamed with dark intent as he descended. He seized the man in one swift motion, pulling him close with an iron grip. Their faces were nearly touching, and the man's eyes widened with terror, his pupils blown wide. It was already too late. Soren's thoughts slithered into the man's mind, sharp and corrosive, a violent chant that seemed to brand itself into the man's consciousness.

The man trembled uncontrollably, his breath ragged, his mind clearly fracturing under the intensity of the forced transfer. When it became clear that he wouldn't retain the chant—his mind too broken to hold it—Soren conjured a slip of paper from thin air. The words scrawled themselves onto the page, an eerie script forming as though written by an unseen hand. Without a word, Soren thrust the note into the man's trembling hands.

Guided entirely by Soren's will, the man moved like a puppet, shuffling toward Sandy's house. I followed, dread pooling in my stomach as I watched Soren's twisted plan unfold.

At Sandy's doorstep, Soren placed the man on the porch and rang the bell, retreating into the shadows with a look of dark amusement. The door creaked open, and the man, shaking violently, began to read from the note in a broken, stammering voice.

"I am unlucky number 9," he said, his voice thin and strained. "I am here to tell you that your plan will not work. I know that the source of all things lives within me, and I am living—and now dying—proof that your plan will not work."
As the final word left the man's lips, Soren ended his life with a flick of his fingers, the motion casual, unfeeling. The man crumpled into Virgilian's arms, his soul slipping free before Soren caught it in his grasp. Without hesitation, Soren rode the essence to the wall once more, leaving death and chaos in his wake.
I watched as the young man dead in Virgilian's arms. I watched as Soren tore his soul from his body and rode it to the Wall. His work was precise, clinical, cruel. Virgilian carried the lifeless body into the house and laid it on the sofa, the cushions sinking under its weight.

"Soren is a monster," Virgilian said, his voice taut with frustration and sorrow. "We never should have included him in this."

"There was no other way," Leopold replied, resigned. "Perhaps his experiments will keep him occupied for a time."

"They won't," I said as I stepped into the room, my voice flat with resignation. "He's built up a tolerance. Even source-aware humans barely faze him anymore. There's no stopping him from doing this. All we can do is scrape together whatever fragments of information his cruelty yields." I let the words hang in the air, the silence pressing down like a weight. "But he's right about one thing: this plan doesn't work. It never has. Nine times we've tried it. Nine times it's failed."

I wasn't sure why I said it—why I felt the need to echo Soren's lie. The words tasted bitter, foul in a way that made my energy crawl. And yet, there I was, speaking it aloud, repeating and almost defending his deceit as if it were my own.

"First of all," Leopold snapped, his tone cutting, "what he's doing is nothing like Virgilian's plan. Secondly, if he's built-up tolerance, then he's killing babies because he wants to, not because he needs to. He's a monster, and it's time he was punished."

"And how, exactly, do we punish him?" Tomas asked, frustrated, threading his voice. "We can't harm each other. We can't hold him in one place without imprisoning ourselves with him. The Source alone can punish him, and it hasn't. What can we do?"

"There is a way," Virgilian said firmly, stepping forward, his expression resolute. "I've thought about it a great deal since Africa. There is a way."

I wasn't really listening. My attention was elsewhere—I could feel Sandy in the house, his presence faint but undeniable. Yet for some reason, I couldn't reach him. My attempts to project to him were blocked.

"How?" Leopold demanded, his eagerness a blade. "Tell me, and I'll deliver it swiftly."

"There's only one punishment that would truly hurt him," Virgilian said, his gaze steady as it landed on me. "You, Caparina. You're the only way. He cares only about you. If you take yourself away from him, he'll suffer."

I froze. The conversation's sudden shift left me reeling. For the briefest moment, my thoughts flicked to Viviana and Leland. And then I realized: I'd be alone.

"I will suffer," I said, my voice trembling as I fought to keep it steady.

"Perhaps you deserve it," Leopold said coldly. "You've let him do whatever he wants."

Inside, I screamed in silent agreement. I know I have. But the confession stayed trapped inside, where it always remained.

"Enough," Virgilian said sharply, raising a hand to silence Leopold. His tone softened as he turned back to me. "You don't have to suffer for him, Caparina. You didn't commit his crimes, but you've been complacent. I'm asking you to distance yourself from him. That is all. Take another partner—there are others who would welcome you."

Another partner? The thought revolted me. No, I thought bitterly, that would dishonor the Source. Viviana and Pascal are already trampling their gift. I will not do the same.

"It’s simple for you, Virgilian," I snapped, my anger rising to the surface. "And for you, Leopold. But Tomas and I—we understand what it means to have the same partner since the beginning."

As the words left my mouth, a sudden unease gripped me. I glanced around and realized Lilith wasn’t in the house. Where was she? Her absence cast a shadow over my thoughts, forcing me to pause, to consider their words more deeply than I wanted to. But the moment passed, and I pressed on, my voice steadier but no less certain.

"There’s no one else for me."

"There's nothing honorable about clinging to a bond purely out of habit," Leopold said, his voice cutting through me. "You've spent months pretending to be something you're not—musical instruments, furniture, anything to keep still. Can't you see that's your way of avoiding him? Suppression breeds dysfunction. You're suppressing your urge to leave him."

"Whose dysfunction caused your separations?" I fired back, sarcasm dripping from my words. "Seraphina? Paisley? Or the other one at home? How many partners have you had, Leopold? How many of them left because of you?"

I couldn't bear the thought of leaving Soren. I'd chosen him—or rather, he'd been chosen for me by the Source itself. Soren would never let me go. He'd torment us both until we shattered.

From the stairway, Sandy's voice broke through. "What is the plan for the dead body on my sofa?" His tone was sharp, his presence suddenly magnetic. I turned to him, relief washing over me. He looked stronger than I'd expected—taller, his hair fuller, his stance firm. But when I tried to project to him again, I felt the same rejection.

"There's a dead body on my sofa," Sandy said again, louder this time. "And I'm the only human in this house. Who do you think will be punished for it?" His gaze locked on me, heavy with accusation.

The room fell silent. The weight of his words was suffocating. I looked away, my defiance faltering.

Virgilian broke the silence, his tone gentler now. "Caparina, no one is asking you to abandon everything. But Soren's actions cannot go unpunished, and you have the power to make a difference."

"Soren will dispose of the body when he returns," I said stiffly, hurt by Sandy's rejection. Then, unable to resist the sting of my own bitterness, I added, "And when he's done, he'll probably dispose of you too."

"You know why his plan isn't working," Sandy shot back, his voice cold. "Everyone does. Even Soren. He's not doing this because he thinks it'll succeed. He's doing it because he's cruel. And you allow it."

Before I could respond, Sandy projected an image to me. It was blurry and incomplete pieces of the Yahudiyah fractured and scattered. The center of the image was missing. But I understood what it meant. The missing piece was Lilith. Only with her contribution would the image resolve itself. And then, perhaps, the Source would speak to us again.

"Has Lilith seen this?" I asked.

"Not yet," Tomas replied.

"Then someone send it to her now," I snapped, impatience lacing my words.

"Second-hand projections," Leopold said with a sigh. "That'll make perfect sense to her." He shook his head. "We've already messaged her. She'll respond to Tomas soon."

"This could all be over if we just had the last piece," I said, turning sharply to Tomas. "What is her reluctance? How bad can her memories of that first trip really be? She was here less than a year, from what I've gathered. What kind of trauma can she possibly be clinging to from a single year? We've been here for eons!"

Tomas didn't answer my questions. Instead, he gave me the same measured, infuriating calm as always. "She'll come," he said, his voice steady. "And we'll complete this project. I'm optimistic about our chances of leaving now. This boy has the capacity to finish what we started. I'm confident he was chosen correctly." He paused, as if weighing his next words. "I've sent her a message. I believe it'll bring her back here. What we need now is patience, someone to deal with the dead body on the sofa before it drives Sandy over the edge, and someone to manage Soren before he commits so many crimes that the Source decides we need another few centuries to learn cooperation."

I frowned, dissatisfied. "How did you get Aryalis to come here?" I asked, my curiosity pulling me out of my frustration. "I thought she'd never leave the Wall."

"We didn't," Leopold interjected, his tone sharp with pride. "The boy came up with the plan. We took him to her."

"All the way to the Wall?" Soren's voice cut in before I could say more.

"How did he survive that trip?" he sneered, sauntering into the room with his usual air of mockery. He leaned casually against the doorframe, his expression coiled and dangerous.

"Don't worry about it," Virgilian said curtly, stepping between Soren and the rest of us. His voice was firm, his posture protective. "He survived. That's all that matters. We're almost complete now."

"You'll behave yourself until this is finished," Leopold said sharply, his gaze locking on Soren with a warning that seemed to suck the air from the room.

Soren's sneer deepened into a venomous smile. "Or what?" he challenged, his tone dripping with contempt. "What will you do to me?"

I felt it the very moment Sandy's thoughts pierced Soren's mind. He was projecting the same image he had shown me, and I watched, fascinated, as Sandy let Soren linger in it, patient and unwavering. After everything he'd endured with us—after all the betrayal, the chaos—he was still going to help us. He was still determined to get us home.

In those seconds, I let myself admit the truth I'd been avoiding. I had fallen in love with Sandy, just as everyone else seemed to. It was undeniable now. But I knew I couldn't hide that from Soren much longer.

I was stunned when Soren, as if silently instructed by Sandy, suddenly removed the lifeless body from the sofa. He carried it out of the room without a word. As soon as he was gone, I tried again to project my thoughts to Sandy. And again, I failed. Crushed, I swallowed the disappointment and forced myself to remain composed. When Soren returned moments later, I buried my feelings even deeper, unwilling to let him see.

"Lilith is the last piece," Sandy said suddenly, breaking the silence.

"Then why don't we just go to her?" Soren asked, irritation sharp in his tone. "You've done it before. Twice, in fact. What's stopping us this time?"

"She'll come to us," Sandy replied with quiet certainty. "In fact, she's already on her way."

"How do you know that?" Virgilian asked, curiosity glinting in his eyes.

"I can feel her," Sandy said calmly. "Just as I can feel all of you."

"If you can feel her, then send your message to her," I urged, trying to keep my tone steady.

Sandy shook his head. "I can't project the way you do. I'm still... tethered to myself. But I can sense the essence of each of you, no matter the distance."

He can sense us, I thought, a flicker of hope igniting. He must have been sensing me too. Maybe he wasn't shutting me out completely. Maybe there was still a chance he could forgive me.

"Impossible," Soren spat, his contempt cutting through the room. "No human can do that. Even we struggle to sense each other without consent. A Yahudiyah must allow their essence to be sensed. No one can bypass that. No one except the Source."

I hesitated. He wasn't wrong. There was no logical explanation for Sandy's abilities. I was deep in thought, questioning why we hadn't tried something like this before, when Soren's voice sliced through my mind.

Do you see her? he projected, his mental link brushing against mine like a sudden chill. That glow… do you see it?

Before I could respond, Sandy's body began to glow.

At first, it was faint—his hands emanating soft tendrils of pale yellow light. But then the glow spread, washing over his entire frame until he seemed to pulse with energy. It grew brighter, sharper, until the whole room felt charged with it.

"Energy manipulation is a rare gift," Sandy said, his voice steady despite the mounting intensity. "Impossible for most humans, yes. But I'm not like most humans. I am far more evolved than any who came before me. I am exactly who you needed me to be. I am the answer to your questions. She will come to us. And when she does, we will finish this. And in the end, all of you will be free."

For a moment, I forgot Soren was in the room. My instinct was to move toward Sandy, to bask in the glow of his presence. Then I remembered Soren, his gaze heavy on me, and forced myself to stay rooted where I stood.

It's the boy, I projected back to Soren, our link thrumming with tension. Why can't you see? It's Sandy—he's affecting us all.

Soren's reply came quickly, sharp and laced with skepticism. Make him prove it. He's powerful, yes, but still human. He'll be weak when we need him to be strong.

I swallowed hard and stepped forward. "You claim to be the answer," I said, my tone careful, measured. "But answers come with consequences. You know how this ends for you. What's to stop you from taking all our power—and changing your mind?"

I hoped the question would appease Soren, or at least buy me a moment to collect myself.

Sandy met my gaze, his expression calm, almost weary. "And do what with it?" he asked softly. "I'm still just a human, Caparina. We all know what happens to humans with extraordinary power. They die. Horribly."

I flinched, his words cutting deeper than I expected. He wasn't wrong. I hadn't signed onto this believing he would survive. But now, with the glow surrounding him and the strength in his voice, I wanted him to. I want you to survive, I thought desperately, projecting the words directly to him despite Soren's presence.

Again, my projection was blocked.

Sandy's voice broke the silence, steady and resigned. "I am not your enemy. My purpose, and my fate, are bound to this mission. I understand that now."

Then, to my surprise, Sandy's thoughts reached all of us at once. His voice cut through every private thread, every secret link, like sunlight breaking through clouds.

You may not believe me yet, but that no longer matters.

I believe you, I thought, seizing the chance to reach him now that the line of communication was open. I blocked Soren out and projected directly to Sandy, my thoughts trembling with the weight of my guilt. I'm so sorry. I am forever ashamed of my actions. Please, forgive me.

And without a word, I felt it. Forgiveness. Pure and complete. It flowed through me, dissolving the knot of shame in my chest.

I glanced at Soren, bracing for his response, but his gaze was fixed somewhere distant, his expression unreadable. It was as if he were staring at something none of us could see.

I let out a breath I hadn't realized I was holding. For once, I was glad for Soren's distraction.

□

Chapter Twelve

The next morning, from my usual perch on the roof, I watched as Sarah Francis returned to us. I wanted to ask her more questions about Viviana and Leland, but I stopped myself. Any discussion of them might draw Soren's attention, and I couldn't risk him knowing what I'd learned—or what I thought of it. So I pushed down my questions and simply watched her enter the house before quietly following her inside.

"We received Tomas's message," she announced, her voice carrying both relief and solemnity. "Lilith is on her way. She has a few final matters to settle before she leaves this planet for good."

It's almost over, I thought for the thousandth time. Lilith would arrive, and this 600,000-year nightmare would finally end.

"Does anyone else have loose ends to tie up?" Virgilian asked, breaking the silence.

"I've got a man trapped in a basement in Austria," Soren said casually, as though remarking on the weather. "But he's probably dead by now."
Sarah Francis turned to him, her eyes narrowing in disbelief. "Why would you leave someone in a basement?" she asked incredulously.

"Of course he has a man trapped in a basement," Leopold interjected, his tone dripping with sarcasm.

"He's not there anymore," I said quietly. "I let him go."

Soren turned his sharp gaze to me, amusement flickering in his eyes. "You let him go? Do you realize you've just unleashed a monster on the world?"

I had, I thought grimly. More than once, it seems. I have a gift for letting monsters roam free.

"So your hostage was a serial killer?" Leopold asked, raising an eyebrow. "And what, you've decided to take up vigilantism now?"

"Oh, I'm no hero," Soren replied smoothly. "I found him before all this human soul business started. Figured he'd make a decent ride when he died."

"Of course you did," Leopold said dryly, shaking his head.

Sarah Francis shot them both a look of frustration. "Can we please focus on what's important? We need to prepare for Lilith's arrival, not get sidetracked by Soren's… hobbies."

But Soren wasn't done. Ignoring Sarah Francis, he turned his attention back to Leopold. "And what were you doing before all this, Leopold? I've heard you on the Wall. You're no innocent. You ride souls just like I do."

"Do not compare us," Leopold growled, his voice low and dangerous. "I don't deny myself the pleasure, but I don't take it the way you do."

Soren sneered, leaning forward as if to savor the fight. "Judge me all you like, brother. But you're no better than I am. Everyone here remembers Le Mans. What was it—83 souls lost? All because you decided beating a human in a race was more important than their safety. And then you rode one of those souls straight to the Wall and wailed like a child for weeks. Where were your morals that day?"

Leopold's face darkened, but Soren pressed on, his voice sharp with accusation. "Have you told the boy about your fondness for human wars? How you love diving into their chaos, riding their leaders, tasting their fear? You're not superior to me. You just wrap your sins in prettier packaging. At least I'm honest about what I am."

"You are honestly a monster," Leopold spat, his voice trembling with rage. "You know everything that happened that day at Le Mans. You know it was your interference that caused me to crash. And you know it's your fault I was wailing on the Wall. Don't speak to me about honor and decency. You've never had either. You've always been what you are—a monster."

Soren's smile widened, his eyes glinting with something feral. "I'm the monster?" he said, incredulous. "You would gladly do me harm right here, right now—your own brother. If you were capable, you'd have ended me centuries ago. And yet you call me the monster." His voice rose, sharp and mocking. "Not one of you here would I ever wish to see destroyed. You're my family, my kin. I know your worth as the Source's first children. But Leopold?" He gestured grandly. "Leopold would see me dead. And why? Because I enjoy handling humans? Because I remind you all that they're nothing more than fleeting sparks? They multiply like rabbits—there's always another. Why the fuss over the few I choose to entertain myself with?"

The room fell silent, the weight of his words pressing down like a storm. I tried to keep my thoughts and emotions as neutral as possible, knowing anything I projected would be fuel for Soren's fire. Everything they said about him was true. I knew it. But I couldn't let myself break—not now. Not when we were so close.

"I've heard enough, Soren," I said finally, my voice steady but firm. "I see their hypocrisy. Humans treat bugs and animals much the same way. But this conversation isn't going to lead us anywhere useful. Let's end it."

Soren's sharp eyes turned to me, and I fought the urge to flinch. I hoped my words sounded like a defense, even though I felt none of it. I didn't want to defend him anymore, but I needed him calm for just a few more hours.

For once, Soren said nothing. His gaze lingered on me for a moment, then drifted away, his thoughts clearly elsewhere. I released a quiet breath, relieved. We were so close to the end. I just needed to hold it together a little longer.

Without warning, Soren exploded from the room, his dark energy trailing behind him like a storm cloud as he launched into the sky. The air seemed lighter the moment he was gone, and I felt my energy relaxed for the first time all morning. His absence was a gift—a temporary reprieve.

As if on cue, Sarah Francis appeared, before I even had a chance to seek her out. She moved with the quiet certainty of someone who had been waiting for this conversation to happen. Her steady gaze met mine, and suddenly, I could no longer hold back.

The questions spilled from me, fast and urgent, as though I had been holding them in for centuries—and maybe, in a way, I had. "How did they do it? How did Viviana and Leland break the bond? How did they... free themselves?"

Sarah Francis didn't hesitate. Her answers came naturally, effortlessly, as though she'd rehearsed them a thousand times or perhaps had known I would ask. Her voice was calm but carried an undercurrent of conviction that struck like a tuning fork, resonating deep within me.

"The truth," she said, her tone unwavering, "is that free will is a gift to all Source-aware beings. Free will is the foundation of independent life from the Source. It is not just yours by chance—it is yours by design." She paused, letting the weight of her words settle. "The Source would never hold you to something you wish to part with. To deny you your will would go against everything the Source stands for."

I stared at her, stunned into silence. Her words seemed to carve through the fog of doubt and fear that had wrapped itself around me for longer than I cared to admit. She believed what she was saying with every ounce of her being, and her certainty was like a flame passed from her to me.

For so long, I had felt trapped—bound to Soren by forces beyond my control, as though our connection was immutable, eternal. But here was Sarah Francis, telling me otherwise, peeling back the lies and assumptions I had clung to for so long.

Free will was mine.

It had always been mine.

The truth of it sank in, filling the cracks in my resolve with something warm and solid. If Viviana and Leland could break their bond—if they could choose freedom—I could too. The Source had given me this life, but it had also given me the choice of how to live it. From this moment forward, I would no longer pretend otherwise.

“I see it now,” I whispered, my voice trembling with a mixture of awe and determination. “I understand.”

Sarah Francis smiled faintly, her expression softening. "Good," she said simply. "Now hold onto that truth, Caparina. You’ll need it."
She lingered for a moment, as though giving me time to let her words settle, and then she turned and moved away, leaving me alone with my thoughts. For the first time in eons, I felt the weight of my choices—and the power in them.

The sky above was empty now, save for the faint trail of energy Soren had left in his wake. His presence had always been so consuming, so impossible to ignore. But now, for the first time, it didn't feel inevitable. I didn't feel tethered to him.

I wasn't free yet—not entirely. But I could see the path to freedom now, clear as the stars.
It wasn't long before Lilith arrived. Like the others, I had been waiting—patiently outwardly, but with a growing, restless anticipation—for her response to the image Sandy had projected. I knew she would want to inspect the boy herself, to examine his body, his mind, and his evolution.

For thousands of years, Lilith had worked tirelessly to develop a "superhuman," someone who could transcend the ordinary limitations of mortality. And here he was. The culmination of her efforts, though not in the way she had ever envisioned. If she hadn't been so grounded in scientific rationale, so steadfast in her belief that our salvation would be rooted in logic and precision, perhaps she could have conceived of what we were all beginning to understand: the answer to our problem was spiritual.

The boy's body was still human—frail, mortal—but his mind, his essence, existed on an entirely different level. Spiritually, he had become something greater, something none of us had anticipated.

Lilith approached Sandy with the controlled demeanor of a scientist inspecting her experiment, but her skepticism bled through the cracks. "We haven't received a single message from the Source since we arrived here—not one word, not a whisper, not a sign. And now you're telling me that you, a boy no one even knew existed until recently, have a direct message from the Creator to us?"

Her tone was sharp, each word laced with disbelief.

"Yes," Sandy replied, his voice calm but confident. "There is a message from the Creator, and I am its bearer. Surprising, I know—but messenger I am, and message I have. Can we finish this so that we may finally read the words of the Creator?"

Lilith's expression darkened, her skepticism hardening into cold determination. "We will finish this now," she said sternly. "But let me be clear, boy: if this turns out to be nothing, if this doesn't bring closure to my time here, you will suffer for it."

Her voice was ice, but her anger wasn't wild—it was precise, controlled, like a scalpel. "I will not allow you to roam this world with my thoughts, Sandy. I can see Virgilian's suffering. I know he wants to save you. I also know that if anyone ends you, it will be him and him alone. But if this is a farce—if this is nothing—he will not stop me from dealing with you myself. Do you understand me?"

I wanted to speak, to defend Sandy. I wanted to tell her that I, too, cared for the boy, that I didn't wish to see him suffer. But I couldn't bring myself to say it. My selfishness hadn't been completely cured—I still wanted to go home.

"You'll have to get in line," Sandy replied calmly, his voice unshaken. "I've received that particular threat several times already. Fear not, Lilith, I mean you no harm. Your thoughts are safe with me; I wouldn't share them even if I lived a hundred years, which, as we all know, I will not. There's no need to dwell on what is already understood. Let us begin, so that this may finally end."

Without waiting for a response, Sandy stepped outside, his movements deliberate, almost serene. He stopped on the patio, where the morning sunlight poured down in golden beams, painting the space with warmth.

"I wish to be in the sunlight for this," he said, turning briefly to face Lilith. "I fear this all began in the dark."

He reclined fully in a folding chair, settling himself as though preparing for a deep rest. Then he gestured for Lilith to join him. She moved forward without hesitation, her presence radiating authority and purpose, and their session began.

Lilith extended her essence toward Sandy, wrapping around him like an invisible tide. Her energy was intoxicating, but she wielded it so gently, so sweetly, that it was impossible to tell if their connection was maternal or something far more intimate. Parent and child? Lovers? Something else entirely? The line between those roles blurred as their connection deepened.

Sandy surrendered to her thoughts, immersing himself completely in the visions she shared. His body responded as though physically experiencing everything she showed him. Tension rippled through him during moments of turmoil. A faint smile curved his lips in moments of joy. His chest heaved with sobs when she offered him her pain. And when the sadness grew too heavy, tears slipped freely down his cheeks.

Hour after hour passed as they remained locked in that mysterious, consuming embrace. The rest of us hovered nearby, watching in tense silence, unwilling to miss a single moment.

We knew Lilith was pouring herself into Sandy—her memories, her regrets, her victories, and her failures. Everything she had ever been was bleeding into him. And Sandy, impossibly, was taking it all. His mortal frame should have faltered, should have crumbled under the weight of her essence, but somehow he held steady, glowing faintly in the sunlight as if it were feeding him.

Watching them, I realized something I hadn't allowed myself to fully admit before: this boy, this unassuming human, was the only being capable of completing what we'd all started. He was both fragile and powerful, mortal and transcendent, and in this moment, he was the most extraordinary creature any of us had ever known.

As though summoned by the moment itself, Soren returned just as Lilith was finishing her session. The sun had set, and the moon now hung high, its pale light spilling across the patio like a silent witness. Lilith pulled away from Sandy at last.

And then Sandy began to rise.

Slowly, his body lifted from the folding chair, the faint golden light surrounding him soft at first but growing steadily brighter. He hovered there, suspended mid-air, his features taut with concentration. The glow around him pulsed, brightening, dimming, then brightening again, each rhythm resonating with a force that seemed to thrum through the very air.

Suddenly, his features softened. His jaw slackened, his lips parting ever so slightly, and the golden glow erupted into something more. The light bathed the patio, spilling out into the night like a second sunrise. It wrapped around us, brushing against us, and I felt it—not just its warmth, but its energy. It pulsed in waves, each one resonating deep within me, a vibration that seemed to echo in my essence.

The world around us blurred. All I could focus on was him—the way his light hummed in harmony with something far beyond us. The air itself seemed alive, trembling with unseen power. The vibrations coursing through me felt almost tangible, as if I could reach out and pluck them like the strings of an instrument. The thought was intoxicating, and for a moment, I let myself drift into it, imagining a symphony woven from Sandy's resonance.

But Virgilian's voice cut through my reverie, snapping me back to reality.

"Can you see the whole message now?" he asked, his tone sharp with anticipation.

"Yes," Sandy replied, his voice steady, though his glow flickered faintly as if the effort were taxing.
And then, all at once, the image appeared—not just to one of us but to all of us, projected directly into our minds. At first, it was blurry, the edges indistinct, like a puzzle still missing its final pieces. But then the image began to sharpen, each fragment slotting into place as though drawn by invisible threads.

We watched as the words came into focus, their meaning settling over us like a whispered revelation. When they were clear, we found ourselves speaking in unison, as if the message demanded to be voiced aloud:

"EVERYTHING HAPPENS FOR A REASON AND IN ITS OWN TIME."

The words hung in the air, reverberating in the silence that followed. No one spoke, each of us reading and rereading the message in our minds, grappling with its weight—or its simplicity.

Finally, the silence was broken.

"You're not going to tell me we did all this for a message we could've pulled out of a fortune cookie," Soren said, his voice dripping with sarcasm. He was glaring up at Sandy's glowing form. "There has to be more. Concentrate, boy. There has to be more."

"No," Virgilian said urgently, stepping forward, his eyes fixed on Sandy with an almost desperate intensity. "Sandy, show us the rest. There is more, isn't there?"

Slowly, Sandy descended to the ground, his glow fading like the last embers of a dying flame. He opened his eyes, exhaustion flickering in them like shadows. "That's all it said," he said quietly, almost sadly. "There is nothing more."

"I knew it," scoffed Soren, throwing up his hands in frustration. "This is a waste of time! The first thing the Source says to us in all this time is 'everything happens for a reason'? Are you serious?"

"And in its own time," Sandy added, his tone calm but resolute, as if the repetition itself held weight.

"It's meaningless!" roared Soren, his anger breaking loose as he glared at Sandy. "It means nothing!"

"No," Leopold countered sharply. "It means everything. It means the Source has a plan, and we just have to trust it. We have to wait."

"Or," Virgilian interjected thoughtfully, "it could mean that everything that has happened triggered what came after. Every action, every choice, set off a chain reaction. The timing of those choices caused things to unfold as they have."

Soren turned on him with a snarl. "What the hell are you even saying? Do you actually know what that means, or are you just talking to hear yourself?"

Virgilian's expression remained calm, though his voice held a faint edge as he tried to explain. "It means that every decision we've made led to this moment. Every event unfolded exactly as it had to. If even one choice had been made at a different time, the outcome would be entirely different. Timing is the key."

"Everything happens for a reason, and in its own time," Sandy repeated, his voice steady and unwavering.

"Say that one more time," Soren growled, stepping forward, his eyes narrowing dangerously. "And I'll have all the reason I need to make something happen to you."

Sandy met his fury with unnerving calm. "It's not time yet," he said simply.

Soren's rage flared. "Of course not! You've taken everyone's memories, delivered your precious message, and now you're stalling. Why isn't it time yet? I think we should finish this now!"

"It's not time yet," Sandy repeated, his tone unshaken.

Soren turned to the rest of us, his anger now seeking allies. "Do you hear him? He's stalling! And we're still trapped here! I think we should end this boy, right now. Who's with me?"

When no one responded, Soren's frustration boiled over. He began pacing, confronting us one by one. "What about you, Tomas? Are you ready to finish this? And you, Lilith—don't tell me you're falling for his nonsense. It's four of us against three. They can't protect him from all of us."

Lilith stepped forward, her gaze sharp and unwavering. "I'm not with you," she said firmly. "And I don't agree."

"Nor I," said Tomas, his voice calm but resolute. "And I won't let you harm him."

Soren's glare swept over them, his fury simmering just beneath the surface. "You're all fools," he spat. "We're wasting time, letting him manipulate us. If no one else will act, I will."

He turned and began advancing on Sandy, but before he could reach him, I stepped between them.

This was my moment. I had known that if it came to this, I would not let Soren touch Sandy. If my purpose was to hold Soren in place for the duration of this human existence, so be it. I would be his cage, and I was ready.

"You will not touch him," I said, my voice firm, my stance unyielding.

Soren's eyes narrowed, his expression darkening. "Oh, great," he sneered, his voice dripping with venom. I could see the storm of emotions flickering across his face—betrayal, disbelief, fury. "You're with them now, too."

He hesitated, his gaze boring into me. The pause was brief, shorter than I expected, as though it didn't take him long to decide I was no longer necessary to him. Finally, he spoke, his tone cold and final.

"It doesn't matter. I'm done with this—done with him." For so long, fear had tethered me to Soren, had kept me doubting myself. But now I saw the truth. I didn't need to fear life without him. I would be fine alone.
"You will roam this world—and every other—alone," I said, my voice steady and strong. "From now until the Source ends our existence, if you lay a hand on that boy. Do you understand me? You will lose all of us."

It wasn't just a threat. It was a chance. I was giving him an opportunity to choose something different, to let go of his violence and anger. I was even willing to forgive everything he had ever done if he could let this go.

But Soren didn't hesitate. "I will do as I please," he growled, his fury undimmed, "and none of you will stop me." He stepped forward again, but before he could get any closer, a protective barrier shimmered to life around Sandy.

The light of the barrier was faint, almost translucent, but its power was undeniable. Soren's advance was halted instantly. He pounded against it, his fists striking the invisible shield in vain, but it didn't budge.

"Everything happens for a reason," Sandy said quietly from within the barrier, his glow returning faintly. "And in its own time. The mission is not complete. We are not done. But I will decide when it's finished. It must be in my time."

Soren's fists fell to his sides, his rage boiled over. "This is pointless!" he roared. "You're delaying the inevitable. He'll be an old man before he decides to set us free!"

The rest of us stood silently, the weight of Sandy's words washing over us like a tidal wave. Relief mingled with awe as we realized Sandy could protect himself, that Soren was no longer a threat to him.

Virgilian stepped closer, his voice quiet but trembling with emotion. "Do you know the time?"

Sandy turned to him, offering a small, sad smile. "Yes," he replied. "I can see my body releasing my soul."

"If we could all see your body releasing your soul now, that would be wonderful," Soren snapped, his voice dripping with sarcasm. I clenched my fists, rage bubbling in me. I had never wanted anything more than for Soren to be silent and gone.

Leopold interrupted, his tone firm but curious. "Can you tell us how much longer we'll need to wait?"

Sandy looked at each of us in turn, his gaze steady, though tinged with sadness. "Your wait is not long, friends. My time is soon. I will not fail you. We are almost complete."

And with that, the barrier faded. Sandy stepped down, brushing past Soren as if he were no more threatening than a gust of wind. "You cannot hurt me," he said softly. "Resist the urge to try."

He turned and walked back into the house, his steps deliberate, his shoulders steady. He entered his room, shutting the door firmly behind him. None of us followed.

Instead, one by one, we drifted apart, catching the wind as we ascended. We floated into the night, each of us reflecting on Sandy’s words, his power, and the weight of what was yet to come.

□

□

Chapter Thirteen

He beat me to Austria. Perhaps because I hadn't realized it was a race. Or perhaps because, for the first time in eons, I was savoring my newfound sense of freedom. I didn't rush. I floated lazily, letting the wind carry me, enjoying the feeling of choosing my own pace for once.

I don't think I understood how destructive he could be—how far he was willing to go—until I arrived at the site where my museum once stood.

The devastation hit me like a physical blow. Every brick, every shutter, every piece of history I had carefully preserved was reduced to smoldering rubble. The air was thick with acrid smoke, the blackened skeleton of the building barely visible through the flames. Emergency crews swarmed the scene, desperately dousing the fire with hoses, their shouts muffled by the crackling inferno. But it was futile. There was nothing left to save.

I hovered above the disaster, watching as flames licked at the remains of what had once been mine. People who had been inside—visitors, staff—were gone. Completely and utterly gone. The building was destroyed so thoroughly that it felt personal, like Soren had wanted to erase every trace of me from this place. Every wall, every doorway, every artifact was ash now. Even the instruments I had collected and cherished over centuries were reduced to dust.

Yet, surprisingly, I wasn't angry.

I felt sorrow for the lives lost, but the building? The instruments? They no longer mattered. My sense of attachment to them had evaporated somewhere along the way. Perhaps it had vanished the moment I realized that my time was my own again. I wasn't tethered to this place, or to Soren. I could go anywhere—find another city, another corner of the world to roam.

I thought of Africa. Vast, ancient, and untouched by Soren's chaos. Perhaps I'd go there, far away from his shadow. The idea comforted me as I drifted over the scene, smoke curling through the night like tendrils of memory.

But as I turned to leave, a thought struck me—a spark of desire I hadn't felt in so long. I didn't care about the museum, but I did want something. Something that was mine. Something Soren hadn't taken.

I traveled to Enns with purpose, my speed now urgent, hoping I would arrive before he had destroyed it too. When I reached the old tower, relief flooded through me: it still stood. Its stone walls, weathered and familiar, rose defiantly against the night sky. I slipped inside, moving quickly through the creaking halls, my energy light as I ascended the winding staircase.

The secret room was exactly as I remembered it, untouched by time or Soren's wrath. My energy quickened as I scanned the space, and there it was—my flute.

It rested exactly where I had left it, as though it had been waiting for me all these years. The first instrument I had ever crafted on this planet, and still intact. I picked it up, running my fingers along the smooth wood, and for a moment, I let myself feel the quiet triumph of holding something that was wholly, undeniably mine.

I felt him before I saw him.

Soren entered the room behind me, his presence pressing against the air like a thundercloud. He didn't speak at first, but I could sense the weight of his expectation. I could already imagine the monologue forming in his mind, the justification for his destruction, the mockery he would hurl my way.

But I didn't give him the satisfaction.

I didn't even turn to look at him. I kept my back to him, ignoring the heavy silence that hung between us. My focus remained on my flute, my fingers gripping it tightly.

Then, without a word, I moved to the window, opened it, and let the cool night air rush over me.

Soren didn't stop me. Maybe he expected me to stay, to engage, to play out the confrontation he had clearly come for. Instead, I stepped into the open air, catching a gust of wind and letting it carry me away.
I didn't look back.

The flute was mine, and that was enough.

I surrendered to the breeze, letting it carry me wherever it pleased. Hours passed, maybe days—time had no meaning when I wasn't paying attention. I just drifted, weightless, my mind blissfully empty. No thoughts, no memories, no plans for the future. It was pure freedom, and I could almost believe it was the happiest I'd ever been.

When Virgilian's message finally reached me—that it was time to return—I floated back to Jacksonville with the same ease that had carried me away. No rush. I knew Sandy would wait for me. I arrived seconds before Soren, surprising us both, though I said nothing as he trailed behind me, sulking like a child.

The others began to gather. I stayed on the roof, in my usual spot, watching from a distance. I didn't want to join their conversation. I was content to remain on the edges, letting their words drift over me like the wind I'd just left.

Seraphina arrived in her human form, which was unusual. I wondered why but didn't ask. Casper and Aquilus came soon after, also clinging to their human forms. No one was surprised. Like Seraphina, the twins had inherited a life shaped by generations of careful breeding, and they were reluctant to leave it behind for an uncertain plan.

"We're all here now," said Soren, his voice sharp with impatience. "Are you going to drag this out, or can we get on with it?"

“This will happen when the boy says it will,” Paisley replied firmly. “And not a moment before.”

“We’re not all here,” added Sandy, his calm voice cutting through the tension. “We await Aryalis.”

Soren groaned, throwing his hands up. “Oh, great. We’re never leaving. He’s stalling again.”

“She never leaves the wall,” I said quietly. “She won’t come. We can’t wait for her.”
But Sandy met my gaze with quiet determination. “She will come,” he said.

Virgilian nodded. “If Sandy says she’s coming, we must wait.”

I believed him. Of course, I did. And though I wasn’t ready for what would happen next, I found myself on the side of waiting. As long as it took.

"You don't want this to happen anyway," Soren accused, rounding on Virgilian. "You're so attached to this human that you'd sacrifice our chance to go home just to keep him."

Virgilian took a deep breath. "What difference does it make if it happens now or later? If this is meant to work, it will. And... you're right. I don't want it to happen. I regret this plan. I want Sandy to live. I want him to survive."

Relief flooded through me, though I kept it to myself, knowing Soren's temper too well.
Seraphina's voice rang out, bright with conviction. "So do I! Don't you see how extraordinary he is? We need more time with him!"

Leopold stepped forward, his quiet agreement carrying weight. "I wish him a longer life. I wish for more time."

I watched Sandy's face as they spoke, searching for his reaction. The love in his eyes was unmistakable, but so was his resolve. Whatever decision would be made here, it wouldn't come from anyone but him.

Soren snapped, frustration spilling over. "I knew this would happen. You gave him power, and now you've fallen under his spell!"

"Silence," I said sharply, cutting across him. My gaze shifted to Sandy. "This isn't our decision. It's his. And he's already made it."

"I have," Sandy said quietly. "Several times, in fact. I'm not stalling. I'm doing what must be done. She will come, and we will wait. In the meantime, I'll listen to each of you in turn. What message would you like to share with your creator before you meet again?"
A stunned silence fell. I hadn't thought about it—what I might say when we returned to the Source. Apparently, neither had anyone else.

Soren broke the silence with a scoff. "Confessions? Who does he think he is, our priest? If the Source is listening, my thoughts are already known."

Leopold stepped forward, his voice steady. "I know exactly what I want to say. I'll go first, if no one objects."

No one did. Sandy led Leopold to a separate room, leaving the rest of us to wait in uneasy silence.
One by one, I watched them go in to speak with Sandy. As I stood outside waiting for my turn, I thought about what I would say to my creator. The words churned in my mind, heavy and unwieldy, because I knew I had so much to say. Too much, perhaps.

When Soren rushed in after Casper, I tensed, instinctively fearing he might harm Sandy. But I reminded myself that Sandy could protect himself. Still, Virgilian and I lingered near the door, uneasy. Since Sandy wouldn't allow Soren to project his thoughts, we overheard his message to the Source. It was exactly what I expected: harsh, unrepentant, and utterly in character. Soren was, and always would be, exactly who he was meant to be. That much was clear.

When Soren finally stormed out, his expression a mask of barely restrained fury, Virgilian slipped into the room to check Sandy for any signs of harm. Finding none, he allowed himself to be ushered out when I entered right behind him. It was clear from my posture and silence that I had no intention of leaving until my turn came.

My message took much longer than anyone else's. What unfolded between Sandy and me was less a simple communiqué to the Source and more of a therapy session—a slow unraveling of centuries of bottled-up thoughts and emotions. Several times, Sandy had to gently remind me that neither he nor the Source was there to judge my actions. But still, my words poured out in an unstoppable torrent.

I confessed to my crimes—not Soren's, but my own. Crimes of selfishness. Of standing by while millions of humans died because I couldn't bring myself to intervene. Of summoning Soren to handle moments I should have confronted myself. Of using him as the weapon for my vengeance, allowing him to reap my anger and fury upon those I deemed unworthy.

I had been no innocent. Far from it. I had been complacent. Worse, in some cases, I had been an active participant. I needed the Source—and Sandy—to know that I understood the full weight of my actions. That I was willing to pay for them.

My words hung heavy in the air, each sentence laden with the gravity of long-held secrets and unspoken fears. I spoke not for forgiveness but for clarity. To own the truth of what I had been and what I had done. When I finally fell silent, the stillness in the room was profound, as if the air itself held its breath.

Sandy stepped forward, sensing the depth of my pain, and allowed himself to be enveloped in my essence. It was a strange and beautiful thing, this act of intangible connection. He held my spirit close, letting me feel his calm, unwavering presence. In that moment, he understood everything—the loneliness, the guilt, the yearning for absolution.

And for the first time in what felt like an eternity, I allowed myself to feel solace. Not forgiveness, not yet. But solace. It was enough.

True to his word, Aryalis arrived.

I was on the roof again, lost in my thoughts, when I saw her scarlet light cutting through the horizon. For a moment, I couldn't believe it. After all this time, she was here. Sandy had summoned her, and she had come. He truly was an extraordinary soul.

Aryalis had never taken human form before, and it showed. She struggled with her shape at first, forming a head and hands, but the rest of her body flickered, shifting in and out of focus. She hovered above the ground, unwilling or unable to touch it. When Sandy entered the patio, he found her surrounded by all of us, our collective awe palpable. None of us were more stunned than Virgilian, whose excitement caused him to shift involuntarily between his human guise and natural state.

Aryalis marveled at Seraphina, Casper, and Aquilus, her golden gaze lingering on their human forms. She studied their shapes with a childlike wonder, trying to mimic the texture of their flesh but never quite succeeding.

"Do you want to give a message to the Source?" Sandy asked her softly.

Aryalis turned to him, and for the first time, her newly-formed face smiled. It was small, tentative, but sincere. Sandy responded with a radiant grin of his own.

She didn't answer with words. Instead, her form began to change, shedding its awkward human guise as she transformed back into her original state. Her song began—a deep, resonant hum that filled the air with vibrating energy. Scarlet lightning crackled around her, the sound building as her form dissolved into rolling clouds. She became a storm: thunderous, electric, beautiful. And then, as quickly as it began, it softened. The storm faded to a gentle breeze, her essence swirling in soft, gray clouds.

No translation was needed. Her message was clear: I have been arrogant, and I have been stubborn. But now, I am humbled.

We were silent, struck by the beauty and finality of her expression. Even Soren, though restless as always, didn't speak at first. But when the stillness lingered, he broke it with his impatience.
"So, now that she's here," he said, his voice sharp, "can we get on with this?"

"Not yet," Lilith interjected calmly. "I still have my message to give."

"And mine," added Virgilian.

"Then hurry up," Soren snapped. "You're all dragging this out."

A wave of glares met his words, and he eventually slunk to a corner, muttering under his breath. Lilith led Sandy into the house for her turn, and I returned to my roof. I played for Sandy while she spoke, my violin's melody drifting down to him like a private concert.

Lilith didn't take as long as I had, but she made her time count. When she emerged, her expression was serene, as though a weight had been lifted.

“It’s your turn, Virgilian,” I said, keeping my tone as even as I could, though I felt the pull of Soren’s impatience in my own words.
Virgilian moved toward the door, but Sandy stopped him gently. “You’ve already given your message to the Source,” Sandy said.

“No,” Virgilian insisted. “I know what I want to say.”

“So do I,” Sandy replied, his voice steady. “Remember, I am your message.”

The realization hit Virgilian like a thunderclap. Sandy was his message. There was nothing left to say.

And that was when it began to fall apart.

“No,” Virgilian stammered, his panic rising. “Not yet. It’s not time yet!”

“Virgilian,” Sandy said, his tone firm yet calm.

"Don't say it!" Virgilian shouted. "We're not ready. Casper, Aquilus—they still need time to shed their forms. We can't—"
Before he could finish, Soren acted.

He transformed into a giant blade—a deadly flash of silver that sliced through the room with terrifying precision. Casper and Aquilus fell instantly, their human bodies crumpling to the ground, lifeless. Seraphina froze, wide-eyed with terror, as the blade swung toward her.

Leopold moved faster than I thought possible, transforming into a wall of steel just as Soren's blade struck. The impact rang out like a bell, ringing loudly for the world to hear.

I stood paralyzed, unable to move, unable to act.

"How dare you!" Seraphina screamed, her voice trembling with rage.

“I’ve wanted to do that for a long time,” Soren said, his voice calm and chilling. “Now, get on with it before I add more to the pile.”

Silence fell, thick with shock and horror.
A yahudiyah wall rose around Sandy, shimmering with determination, each of us pouring our strength into it to shield him from Soren. The energy crackled with purpose, unyielding and immovable. Then, I heard Sandy’s voice in my mind, soft but resolute: Step away from the wall and play for me.

For a moment, I hesitated, caught between duty and his command. But his voice carried a certainty I couldn’t refuse. Slowly, I stepped back, letting go of the wall’s protective energy.

With a wave of my hand, I conjured my violin. The familiar weight of it rested against my shoulder, the bow steady in my hand. I closed my eyes and began to play—not just for Sandy, but for all of them. The music poured out of me, weaving through the room like a living thing, carrying every ounce of my fear, hope, and love. It wasn't just a melody; it was a story, a plea, a promise.

The notes rang out like the opening of a grand concert, soaring and commanding, yet laced with an aching tenderness. Each stroke of the bow seemed to connect us all, binding us together in a fragile moment of shared humanity.

I played for Sandy, pouring everything I had into the melody, knowing deep in my soul it was the last song I would ever give him. Each note was a farewell, a tribute, and a final act of devotion.

Soren prowled like a caged predator, his movements sharp and impatient, as though my music was nothing more than an irritating hum to him. He didn't stop, didn't flinch. His focus was locked on Sandy, his frustration radiating like a storm as he pushed against the barrier, still trying to reach him.

Then, Sandy's voice broke through it all—calm, steady, and impossibly clear.

"Enough," he said from behind the shimmering yahudiyah wall, his words cutting through the tension like a blade. The music faltered on my bow as his tone reached me.

"The time is now."

"No!" Virgilian cried, his voice breaking. "Please, don't let it end like this!"

But it was already happening. Sarah Francis stepped forward, her light shining so brightly that no one could stop her—not that they would have tried. She enveloped Sandy gently, her essence merging with his. Together, they rose, her tendrils carrying him upward as his body fell limp. His soul was in her grasp now.

I stopped playing. I felt his death. Sandy was gone.

As Sarah Francis spread herself wide, she extended her glowing tendrils to the rest of us. I clung to her light as she carried me upward, away from the chaos. Below, I saw Sandy's body fall into Leopold's waiting arms. Seraphina stood beside him, but I didn't question why they stayed. It wasn't my concern anymore.

We rose higher, toward the wall. For a fleeting moment, I wondered about Lilith's pink light, which had drifted away, but I reminded myself again: it wasn't my concern.

Moments later, we passed through the wall as if it had never existed, dissolving into something far beyond its reach. I caught a glimpse of Soren breaking away from himself, his attention splintering as he sent a message back to Earth. For a fleeting moment, curiosity flickered in me—who was it for? What was the message? But the thought evaporated just as quickly as it had come, replaced by the reminder that it didn't matter anymore. Soren, his schemes, his endless machinations—none of it was my concern now.

As we moved further, I felt the weight of everything slip away: Earth, Soren, the past. All the burdens I'd carried for so long unraveled and drifted into nothingness. I was free.

For the first time in an eternity, I was free.